Doorways to the Unseen 12

6 Tales of Terror and Suspense

James Dermond

Ambages Books

This book is a work of fiction. The names, characters, organizations, places, events, and dialogue are either products of the author's imagination or are used in a fictitious manner.

ISBN 978-1-946038-11-1

Cover art by Jeff Purnawan

"Be silent in that solitude, Which is not loneliness—for then The spirits of the dead who stood In life before thee are again In death around thee—and their will Shall overshadow thee: be still."

- "Spirits of the Dead" by Edgar Allan Poe

Contents

The Insatiable	1
The Dhampir	23
The Underworld	39
Spirits of the Dead – The Third Story	63
Cirque des Plus Grands Mystères	81
Doorways to the Unseen	103
About the Author	113
Postscript	115

The Insatiable

Preston Winscott folded his copy of *The Times*, having just read the front-page news. There had been another murder at the city docks, this one as gruesome as the last. For months, a vicious killer had terrorized the city, slaying apparently at random. The victims all occupied lower social strata but otherwise had nothing in common. All had been found with missing organs and all had died with their throats ripped out. The police had no suspects and no leads, so the killer remained at large.

"You, young Winscott, have you read about the latest homicide down by the docks?" Gerald Hoskins approached Winscott as he sat in their club's drawing room on one of its palatial leather seats. Winscott had recently been inducted into the gentlemen's society of which they were both members. "This time, it was a street hawker," Hoskins continued, in his characteristic gruff manner. "The poor boy was found lying among his newspapers and wares. A bloody mess, like the others."

"Yes, Mr. Hoskins, I'm afraid I have," Winscott replied as he looked up at the older man. "This is the fourth victim now, isn't it?" Hoskins was a club officer and a close confidant of its founder, John Fallada. "*The Times* has been following the case. It's all been very sensational."

"I hope they catch him soon. Whomever it is is a madman and deserves to hang," Hoskins said pointedly. He then walked away, seating himself among several other society members engaged in riotous conversation, their copies of *The Times* in hand or nearby.

Winscott had joined the Argentum Club to socialize with others who shared his interest in natural science and the arts. A newly graduated medical doctor, Winscott was a man of relatively modest means but had nonetheless been inducted by the members with unanimous support. Owing to his quick mind and encyclopedic knowledge of the biological sciences, Winscott had won entry into the society where many others of his age and social standing had been turned away.

Taking out his pocket watch, Winscott checked the time: he needed to be back at the surgery in one hour. Winscott left the club and walked several blocks to a horse-drawn tram. He rode it back to the city hospital where he was employed. His mentor at the hospital, Doctor Arthur Burton, was waiting there for him.

"Doctor Winscott, so good of you to join us. You're late." Doctor Burton stood with the trainees in the surgery, their patient under anesthesia lying between them on the table. "You'll only need observe; this is a procedure you haven't yet needed to attempt outside of your studies."

The room reeked of bodily fluids. *The man on the table must have an infected limb*, Winscott decided. The patient was aged and bare under the white cloth that covered his midsection. Winscott placed a handkerchief over his nose and watched as a trainee doctor opened a leg wound, yellowish-white pus oozing forth from it. A second trainee doctor gagged, his mouth covered by a hanky.

After their session, Doctor Burton asked Winscott to meet him in his offices adjoining the surgical room. "Next time, you'll have to perform the same procedure by yourself while under my observation," Doctor Burton told him.

"The medical profession has made great progress these last few decades, I'm happy to say," Doctor Burton enthused. "That man would have likely lost his limb under unspeakable agony if we hadn't been able to sedate him and treat the inflammation." Doctor Burton slipped a vest and suit coat over his clean linen shirt before sitting.

"Medical school opened my eyes to these advances, Doctor Burton. I can only imagine what this new century may bring," Winscott said warmly, having already seated himself before Doctor Burton's desk.

Doctor Burton seemed concerned, as if his mind carried a heavy weight. "Winscott, you're aware of these terrible murders taking place around the city docks, are you not? The victims have all been found mutilated." Doctor Burton paused, peering into Winscott's face as if waiting for his reply.

"Why, yes, of course, Doctor Burton. The entire city is on edge over the homicides. I've been reading *The Times* for daily updates." Winscott thought it odd that Doctor Burton would even ask; everyone had heard of these murders. They were without precedent in the city's recent history.

"You're right. I only wanted to put into context what I'm about to tell you," Doctor Burton said, a hint of trepidation entering his voice. "I've been in contact with the commissioner at Scotland Yard and the detectives assigned to the case. Certain details have been made available to the newspapers, while others haven't. As head surgeon here, I've helped perform the autopsies on the deceased victims in each instance." Doctor Burton was now noticeably uncomfortable—a slight sheen of sweat glimmered on his forehead, and he kneaded his fingers into his palms.

Winscott frowned, afraid of where the conversation was going. "The articles have mentioned organs extracted from those killed, which is bizarre in and of itself," Winscott remarked, "but what else could have been left out if the police were willing to divulge such a morbid particular?"

"The police could only hide so much about the conditions of the bodies as the victims' remains were found by members of the public. However, the autopsies I completed on the dead have revealed a horrifying detail: the missing organs were likely eaten—directly from the wounds of the deceased." Doctor Burton's previously worried expression became one of visceral disgust.

"Why, that's horrible," Winscott blurted out. "So, the police are dealing with not only a killer but a cannibal as well?"

"Yes, it appears so. The detectives considered consulting an alienist, but for now they want to know if we have ever found any bodies that had been defiled like this. The remains dredged up from around the docks area often end up here," Doctor Burton explained, relieved to finally tell another the terrible secret he had been holding close to his chest.

"So, if I may ask, why are you telling me this, Doctor Burton? I would surmise that this is information the police would want to keep hidden from the public. As head of surgery, you should be able to let the police know what they need to help solve the murders." Winscott didn't want to seem insubordinate, but he was surprised Doctor Burton would relate any of this to him at all.

"Winscott, the police have reason to believe the murderer is possibly connected to the society you've recently joined, the Argentum Club," Doctor Burton revealed. "The only witness has been kept out of the papers in the hopes the killer will become overconfident and careless. The witness claims to have seen a man leave the docks near the scene of a killing before returning to your club. It was the most recent murder, from last week."

"Who is the witness that the police are protecting?" Winscott queried, now intrigued by all of this, even though his previous fear was not yet relinquished.

"No name was provided to me, of course, but the witness is another street hawker, a companion of the young boy who was slain," Doctor Burton confided. "He followed a man he described as 'dressed as a fine gentleman'—that is, wearing a top hat and cape. The man headed through the night streets to the back of the Argentum Club. The man slipped through a door behind the club, apparently.

"On this particular night, a heavy fog had set in, preventing the boy from seeing more than how the man was dressed," Doctor Burton continued. "The boy later reported his dead friend to the police. He had heard screaming, but by the time he arrived, there was only the suspicious gentleman leaving an alley nearby. As you can imagine, a gentleman would be quite out of place in that down-market part of town."

"So, what do the police want me to do? You've just described nearly every member of the club: 'a top hat and cape.' There must be a few hundred members now. The club has grown so much over the last twenty years." Winscott seemed rather proud as he relayed this fact.

"And I'm sure much of that is due to the prominence of your club's founder, Mr. Fallada," Doctor Burton said plainly. "That's the other issue: the police only have the word of a young boy, and an impoverished one at that. They can't search the club and question its members based on the unsubstantiated accusation of an urchin.

"Besides, Mr. Fallada is quite wealthy—he could possibly buy immunity for one of his members unless a compelling case is leveled against him. It's all just too much for the police to manage themselves, and this is their only lead, however tenuous. If you have any suspicions or observe anything, they want to know about it." Doctor Burton then gave Winscott a hint of a smile, hoping to gain his assent.

"Well, I'll do what I can. I'm still a junior member and I'm not privy to all that much. If I see or hear anything dodgy, I'll tell you right away." Winscott hoped Doctor Burton would be pleased with this answer and then just forget about the entire matter. The idea that one of the Argentum Club members, all accomplished men in their respective fields, was stalking the city docks, slaughtering the downtrodden, and then cannibalizing their remains seemed preposterous.

"By the way: *Fallada*. What kind of name is that? He's certainly not a member of the gentry. Is Mr. Fallada a foreigner?" Doctor Burton was polite when he said this but seemed more than simply curious.

"He has foreign roots, I'm told, but was born here," Winscott replied, casually repeating what he had heard from club members. "It seems he's descended from an Iberian princeling or something of the sort. His family made their fortune in precious metals generations back."

After attending to patients and completing his rounds, Winscott left the hospital later that evening. The fog was thick in the city streets, rolling past him as he walked to his residence nearby. *If the killer is a member of the Argentum Club, who might it be?* pondered Winscott, brushing the idea from his mind almost as soon as he thought of it.

***

The crowd was larger than Winscott had supposed it would be. Perhaps fifty or more people were facing the low stage: nearly a packed house. Winscott was skeptical about being here at all, let alone about the likelihood of learning anything worthwhile. His fellow member of the Argentum Club, Foster, had invited him to this demonstration on mesmerism. Winscott regretted attending as soon as he sat down near the stage, his chair in the front row.

"There you are, Winscott." Foster stood in the room's threshold, dressed in his winter suit. "I'm so glad you could make it. I'm sure you won't be disappointed." All smiles, Foster took the empty seat next to Winscott and then scanned the room behind them. "Quite a turnout. The mesmerist should be here soon."

"Why did I let you invite me here, Foster? And why do you believe in this fashionable nonsense," Winscott lamented, asking the second question in a lower tone of voice. "Aren't you a naturalist? You should be pressing butterflies, not obsessing over this bunk."

A woman sitting behind Winscott whispered sharply to her male companion as if angered by the opinion Winscott had just expressed.

"Just have an open mind, Winscott. Once you witness a demonstration of mesmerism, you'll be completely convinced of its veracity." Foster then stood to greet someone sitting nearby. Several minutes passed before he returned, nearly levitating with anticipation.

Soon, a man arrived on stage, smartly dressed and carrying a compact leather briefcase. He placed the briefcase on the table at the stage's center. On either side of the table stood a plush velvet chair, much like those used by the audience.

The man opened the briefcase and took out several items he then placed on the table, too small to be seen clearly from where Winscott was seated. The man then turned to the assembly and raised his arms in welcome.

"Good evening, ladies and gentlemen. I'm so glad that you have come. My name is Alexander Beaumont. I was both a protégé and close confidant of the late Madame Obolensky, as well as a senior member of her Society of Harmony. Her society for the inquiry into spiritual matters and life after death continues after her recent and most unfortunate demise.

"This evening, I will provide a demonstration of the enlightened science of mesmerism, of which both Madame Obolensky and I are—were, in her case—ardent devotees. The practical application of mesmerism can cure physical ailments, heal the broken mind, and reveal secrets of which even the subject may be unaware.

"All I ask for is a volunteer from the audience, chosen at random, who is willing to show everyone gathered here today the power of this technique and demonstrate what it can do for the healthy and afflicted alike."

A young woman in the audience stood up immediately, calling out, "Me, Mr. Beaumont. I volunteer." She then strode confidently toward the stage and stood next to Beaumont, waiting for permission to take the seat next to the table.

Beaumont seemed surprised, as if he hadn't anticipated such an eager response. "All right then, Miss. What's your name, if I may ask?"

The young lady replied enthusiastically, "Penelope Matthews, at your service."

The audience chortled in response, enamored at this fetching young girl's bravado.

"Pleased to make your acquittance, Miss Matthews. Now, please, remove your fine hat—place it on the table here—and sit very still in this chair." Beaumont then reached for one of the objects he had left on the table earlier.

Penelope seated herself and Beaumont took the other chair, facing her. He produced a coin pendant on a silver chain which dangled as he held it. "Relax and breathe out slowly, Miss Matthews. I'm going to mesmerize you with this charm. You will go to sleep, and when you wake, you will remember none of this. But when I tell you to wake up, you'll awaken instantly."

Staring fixedly at the oscillating pendant, Penelope became quickly and visibly heavy-lidded as the charm swayed rhythmically in Beaumont's grasp. She slowly entered a state of repose, and the audience hushed as they watched, spellbound.

Winscott whispered softly to Foster, "What's that necklace he's using? It looks ancient."

"I don't know," Foster murmured. "The coin on the chain might be from a museum."

"Now, Miss Matthews, you are asleep," said Beaumont in a calm, steady voice. "Please, tell me, are you asleep, Miss Matthews?"

Penelope answered Beaumont in a faraway voice, "Yes, I am asleep."

A low gasp rippled through the audience as they heard her reply.

"Good. Miss Matthews, we're going to go back into your past: to any place or time before this one. Allow your mind to wander and find a memory. Once you've found it, please tell me what it is and where you are." Beaumont still held the silvery pendant, but it was now hanging loosely from his hand.

Penelope's head began to turn back and forth as it rested against the back of the chair. Her lips began to move until, steadily, sounds emerged. "I'm somewhere in a dark forest. I'm chasing something, running very fast."

Beaumont remained calm. "Miss Matthews, please tell us more. Is there anyone with you? What are you chasing in those woods?"

"I'm not myself... I'm something else," Penelope replied, her voice sharpening, growing loud and shrill. "There are wolves around me. Large black wolves. It's night, and we're hunting."

There were audible gasps from the audience. Winscott looked around; many seemed visibly startled or upset.

Beaumont was taken aback, as if this was entirely unexpected. "Miss Matthews, are you sure that this is your memory and not just a bad dream? How do you know that this is you?"

Penelope's head turned back and forth as before. Abruptly, she stopped. Her eyes shot open. Her pupils were gone, her irises now completely white, as if she were blind. Penelope then growled in an animalistic voice, "Let me show you."

Leaping forward from her chair, Penelope grabbed Beaumont by his throat, sending them both tumbling to the stage floor in a clatter. Snarling savagely, Penelope clawed at Beaumont's eyes and bit at his face, the stunned Beaumont defenseless as he lay sprawled on his back.

Men from the audience rushed to Beaumont's aid while others ran screaming from the conference room. One woman fell to the floor in a faint. Three men had to pull Penelope from Beaumont, his face bloodied as she flailed wildly.

Beaumont climbed to his feet and cried, "Penelope, you will wake now!" Penelope abruptly went limp in the arms of the men who had restrained her. She slowly opened her eyes and, seeing the blood covering Beaumont's face, recoiled in disbelief.

Wiping his face with a cloth handkerchief, Beaumont winced and then asked the men to let go of Penelope.

"Are you sure, sir? This madwoman nearly killed you." The bearded man in a black suit held Penelope cautiously, a hand under one of her arms.

"Miss Matthews isn't at fault. The mesmerism session must've gone awry. Please, place her in the chair and let her go. She is her sweet young self again." Beaumont examined his face with his fingers, touching shallow slash wounds and wincing in pain once more.

The men carefully put Penelope back in her chair by the table and stood guard nearby. Penelope looked about the room before burying her face in her hands, sobbing uncontrollably.

Winscott and Foster had watched all of this unfold, too surprised to have intervened in time. Winscott saw the silver coin pendant lying on the floor near the stage, cast aside during the utter chaos that had unfolded mere moments before. The image on the silver coin was that of a she-wolf suckling her two cubs. Before anyone could see him, Winscott snatched up the pendant and quickly left the room.

***

"That was quite a ruckus at the Arts Club. One of their open conferences for discerning members of the public, I presume." Doctor Burton spoke to Winscott from behind his desk, having recently returned from the surgery. His mood seemed to have improved since their last encounter, when he had first told Winscott about the cannibal killer.

"That poor woman who went mad is in an asylum now, at least temporarily. And we both know what it's like in there." Winscott thought back to that evening, disquieted at the shocking scene he had witnessed.

"Well, Winscott, do you have anything for the police? I mean, do you have any suspects at the Argentum Club so far? Even anything uncertain you've seen?" Doctor Burton seemed hopeful.

"No, nothing," Winscott replied offhandedly. "I think the police may have been led astray by that street urchin. There hasn't been another murder by the docks since last month and I've found no reason to suspect anyone at the club." Winscott believed this answer would satisfy Doctor Burton, finally.

"You know, the police detective working on the case brought something quite interesting to my attention," Doctor Burton said carefully, his eyebrows rising as he spoke. "Every time there's been a murder by the docks, it's been on a night when the moon was full. The victims were found early that morning or during the day, but it seems the murders were done under the moon's full illumination. The newspapers haven't yet picked up on this pattern."

Winscott appeared puzzled. "When's the next full moon?"

Doctor Burton replied, "On Christmas Day. Will there be a gathering at your social club then?"

"Yes, but likely early in the evening," Winscott answered. "Married members will be at home with their families soon afterward. Since I'm still a bachelor, I'll probably remain longer. There will likely be a few revelers staying late, with nowhere else to go."

"Stay and see if you notice anyone leaving late," Doctor Burton requested, then becoming quiet for a moment as if unsure whether to ask some troubling question. Finally, he said, "Can you tell me more about Fallada?"

"Why do you ask? Do you suspect him?" Winscott again seemed puzzled.

"No, I don't suspect anyone," Doctor Burton reassured Winscott. "It's just that there's more to his background than most realize, including your club members. There are reasons to believe he's a naturalized citizen, not native-born, and that his family has rather unsavory connections—more than most might suspect. I have contacts in the Civil Service, and they did the necessary research for me."

"I've only met Mr. Fallada once," Winscott stated distantly, remembering the past encounter. "When I was first inducted into the society. He was a very well-spoken, charming man, quite supportive of my candidacy. But he's not really there all that much, it seems. Generally, it's Mr. Hoskins who keeps things running."

"Well, keep an eye on Mr. Hoskins as well," Doctor Burton urged. "We'll see if anything comes of Mr. Fallada soon. The police are going to stake out the docks on Christmas Day and station an officer outside of the Argentum Club. But the docks are such a large space, and they only have so many men.

"If you see Mr. Fallada or anyone else leave the club alone late that night, please follow him and see where he goes," Doctor Burton further enjoined, his voice becoming low. "The police can't spare any more men on what is only guesswork at the moment. They'll be working undercover, not in uniform."

***

Walking up the steps to the Argentum Club's front doors, Winscott noted the busy street beyond. Tonight, there would be a Christmas social, and Winscott would see John Fallada and many other members of the club in one place.

A magnificent Christmas tree stood in the drawing room's center, the room's rich furniture having been moved aside to make space for it. Winscott observed club members beginning to congregate. Many were served drinks from trays by demure waiters, and all spoke haltingly among themselves. Winscott reached into his suit breast pocket and touched the silver pendant, still unsure whether it was to blame for that young woman's transformation into a rabid beast.

Winscott continued surveying the drawing-room, pondering who the killer might be, assuming he was here at all. Most club members were entirely unassuming, so it did little good speculating on their criminal natures without evidence. These men possessed no peculiarities that might implicate them in the murders. As for those who did stand out, they hardly seemed the murderous sort. There were several, however, who did warrant consideration—and they were at the Christmas party tonight.

There was Mr. Stevenson, who had a very unpleasant personality and had often made unfavorable comments about "the lower classes." But violent enough to have committed these murders? Almost unbelievable.

Then there was Mr. Chapman, who was quite a suspicious character, making queer pronouncements and slinking about at gatherings. But he was more of an eccentric and not someone who could be considered dangerous. Just an oddball.

And then there was Mr. Hoskins. Short-tempered, coarse to the point of rudeness at times, and always keeping irregular hours. The last one to leave the club at night, almost without fail, but usually to his waiting carriage. It wasn't unimaginable that he could take a life but, again, the carnage around the docks was beyond what even a man like Mr. Hoskins was capable of. *There's probably no killer here at all*, decided Winscott.

Winscott then saw Mr. Fallada enter the room—it was only the second time he had seen him in person. Silver-haired and wearing a charcoal-gray suit, Fallada beamed as he strode in, greeting club members earnestly and then joining Mr. Hoskins near the bar cart. He leaned in to speak into Mr. Hoskin's ear for a moment, then left to converse with someone else.

As the early evening hours passed, club members began to leave for their homes and private family celebrations. Mr. Fallada approached Winscott to welcome him. "Winscott, it's so good of you to make an appearance at our annual Christmas soirée. The new members often consider this event optional. I can assure you that it is not."

"I'm pleased to be here, Mr. Fallada. I wouldn't have missed the club's Christmas social for anything." Winscott tried to smile as Fallada shook his hand, but the older man's intensely steady gaze made Winscott uncomfortable. Shooting a quick glance away from Winscott's face and down toward his chest, Fallada then walked away without saying another word.

Foster had been watching the pair. He walked up from behind Winscott and said, "So, how are you, old boy?" and slapped him on the back. "I haven't seen you since the debacle at the Arts Club. I hope you don't blame me for what happened."

"No, not at all. No one could have seen that coming. I'm still just a bit worried about the girl, that's all." Winscott wanted to give Foster his attention, but he was still distracted by his unsettling exchange with Fallada only moments ago.

"Her parents should be able to extricate her from the asylum soon. As I understand it, the alienists want to ensure she's not a threat before releasing her." Foster gave a tight smile. "So! Any plans for later this evening?"

"I think I'm going to stay late here. Enjoy the holiday festivities and all that." Winscott was able to smile this time—he hoped that would be enough to make Foster leave him alone.

"There won't be too many left later tonight. Only old Hoskins and the other hangers-on. See you around the club again soon, what?" Foster turned his back and then made his way toward the open doors leading to the foyer.

The hours passed, and club members continued to leave, with Winscott finally standing near the Christmas tree by himself. Mummers could be heard out in the street going from door to door, bringing seasonal cheer:

We wish you a merry Christmas,

And a happy New Year,

A pantry full of good roast beef,

And barrels full of beer.

As the mummers' caroling faded away, Winscott noticed Hoskins pass through a curtain that led up a small flight of stairs to the club officers' personal chambers. Rank-and-file society members were only allowed on the club's second floor for induction ceremonies and other official matters.

What could Hoskins be doing? Winscott wondered as he watched his acquaintance pull the crimson red curtain aside, briefly revealing the steps leading up, and then vanish. *I've only ever seen him leave the club through the front doors and then take his carriage. And nothing's going on upstairs this late, that's for sure.*

Thinking quickly, Winscott decided to take a chance. He looked around and, confident the coast was clear, casually strolled toward the red curtain. With a final glance over his shoulder, he parted it and slipped inside. The sound of Hoskins' footsteps echoed from the floor above, and Winscott heard a door close.

The upstairs club room was empty, with the doors to the small private chambers along its hallway shut. *The door sounded like it was closed back here*, Winscott considered. He walked down a cramped staircase leading to a narrow back door. It was locked, and Winscott slid the bar loose before quietly cracking the door open and slipping his head out.

Soup-like fog rolled over the cobblestone street connected to the alleyway. The light from the full-risen moon remained mostly obscured by clouds drifting overhead, but nonetheless Winscott spied the silhouette of Hoskins walking slowly into the night, alone. Stepping into the alley, Winscott shut the door behind him and began following Hoskins at a distance.

Winscott skirted the glow of gaslight streetlamps, keeping to the shadows. Eventually, Hoskins entered an alley close to the docks district. Winscott stopped across the street, sheltered by an unlit shop's threshold. He hoped Hoskins would come out soon.

Instead, a guttural growl pierced the night, followed by a hideous cry and, finally, the sound of flesh being rended. Winscott remained tightly hidden as the screaming continued, panicked that he had found the real killer.

The screaming stopped and from the alley emerged a man dressed in a top hat and cape. He paused for a moment, looking both ways down the empty street. The man then slipped out of view, disappearing into the thick fog which billowed around him.

Hesitating, Winscott wondered if he should check the alley Hoskins had entered, almost sure of what he would find. *A dead end*, he thought, gulping, *no other way out*. He cautiously walked across the now silent street and peered into the gloomy alleyway, seeing what looked like mangled human remains among the dustbins and debris.

Hoskins, why him? Why was he out here all by himself? Winscott gasped as he began to retrace his steps, lost otherwise, following street signs and city landmarks back to the Argentum Club. He found the backdoor unlocked and stepped inside, standing in the dark space at the bottom of the stairs.

A light shone from the floor above. The stairway creaked as Winscott ascended, feeling both curious and afraid. It was past midnight; who could be at the club this late?

One of the chamber doors was cracked open, the room's light pouring out into the hallway. Winscott quietly moved toward the door, pausing a few paces from the entrance.

He heard a voice, Fallada's: "Please come in, young Winscott. I know that you're there."

Winscott froze in place, his legs made of stone.

"Don't just stand there in the hallway. Please do come in."

The door creaked open wider, as if moved by unseen hands. Winscott peeked inside and saw Fallada slipping on his suit coat, grinning. "Yes, come in. I've been waiting for you."

Winscott stepped inside. Fallada stood in front of him at his desk, wearing the same gray suit as earlier in the evening.

"I know you have the amulet. Please give it to me," Fallada requested, still grinning, the upright palm of his hand now outstretched.

"What happened to Hoskins? Was that you in the alley tonight?" Winscott sputtered in response, overwhelmed by what was happening to him.

"Hoskins had to be removed, I'm afraid. He knew too much about what happened with Madame Obolensky. Even after her death, she still has many devoted followers, and they were beginning to grow suspicious." Fallada let his hand fall to his side.

"Madame Obolensky? Were you responsible for her death?" Fear was starting to overcome Winscott, but he remained steadfast. He thought his life might depend on it.

"Yes. But 'Madame Obolensky' was actually a pseudonym. Her accent, as well as her entire persona, were affected. The woman was a charlatan and a quite well-paid one. But she *did* have this in her possession before I took it from her." Fallada reached into his breast pocket and produced a silver pendant, identical to the one recovered by Winscott at the mesmerism session.

"The old fraud had no idea what she really had at her bosom. But I did. Using this sacred artifact to perform mere parlor tricks . . ." Fallada shook his head, his face showing obvious disgust.

"You're the killer, Fallada," Winscott said firmly, angered that he could have been led into this web of deceit. "The police—they will corner you and eventually bring you to justice. But your charm, what does it do for its owner? Why would you kill to get it from that mystic?"

"This charm, as you call it, was forged in fire by my ancestors many generations ago. Indestructible, except in the place where it was created. The pendant was then lost for centuries, but we made every effort to find it. When we recently learned the silver pendant was held by Madame Obolensky, I took the necessary action," Fallada said, his expression gloating.

"But what does it give its user, you ask? Power. And immortality. To be free, and to be powerful, and, of course, to live forever. I am and will be forever, a true apex predator," Fallada declared, his eyes wide with exhilaration. "Now, if you please, Winscott, your silver pendant.

As I said, I know you have it." Fallada grinned and stretched out his hand once more.

"How can we both have the pendant?" Winscott asked, panting, backing away as he touched his suit breast pocket. "Or is mine a copy?"

"A forgery, yes. Created by Madame Obolensky's disciples. But apparently with properties of the original, as the Arts Club found out. Now, please . . ." Fallada took a step forward, no longer grinning.

Winscott turned as if to run, but Fallada's words held him rooted to the spot. "Oh, don't try to leave, young Winscott. The outside doors are all locked. I've seen to that. You won't be getting out of here—not alive, at least."

The silver pendant in Winscott's suit pocket glowed with an eerie blue light, the radiance visible even from beneath the fabric. Fallada donned his own silver pendant, a heavy sweat forming across his brow.

"No one will ever find you, Winscott," Fallada taunted, his voice now low and growling. "Not that there'll be much of you left." Fallada dropped to his hands and knees, his suit ripping at its seams as he fluidly transformed into an enormous silver-and-gray-furred wolf. The chamber door then shut on Winscott as if of its own volition, blocking his escape.

The slavering beast stalked toward Winscott from across the room. Instinctively, Winscott reached into his suit pocket and held out the pendant for protection, its unearthly light intensifying as he did.

A candescent, blue-hued fog began to seep under the closed door, engulfing the floor as the gray wolf drew closer. Fallada stopped in his—its—tracks and began to snarl, as if under attack from the spectral mists. Other wolves formed from within the fog, snapping and biting at the gray wolf. Ghostly howls echoed from the walls of the room as more wolves materialized in the vapor and besieged their beleaguered opponent.

Fallada was seized on all sides. The fog wolves pounced, clawed, bared their teeth, and finally brought down the monstrous gray wolf. The still, nude form of a man was left lying on the carpeted floor as the mists receded. Winscott leaned over Fallada's corpse, removing the silver pendant from around his neck.

***

"You're not far, *señor*. You are near the castle. It's only a few miles north from here." The farmer had stopped his mule-drawn cart when Winscott hailed him. Winscott folded his map, thanked the man, and continued his journey on foot up the dusty and pitted road. He was glad to have finally found a local who could understand him this far from the city.

The imposing castle rose on the horizon, its towers jutting against a clear, blue, cloud-strewn sky. Winscott touched his shirt pocket, feeling the outline of the two pendants that rested therein. Soon, the silver pendants would be returned to the earth from which they had first been shaped, no longer the creations of men or of gods.

The Dhampir

The door was unlocked, which Wes hadn't expected. Unneeded for the moment, he put the spare key back into the pocket of his jeans for safekeeping. He opened the cabin's peeling, weather-beaten entryway, revealing a musty, neglected interior.

A single square room made up the entire space within. Thick curtains had been pulled over the cabin's handful of grimy windows and soft light spilled through several threadbare spots, illuminating the otherwise darkish place.

Wes strode to the room's center, dropping his canvas duffel bag onto the creaking floor. He hastily looked about as if searching for something. There wasn't much furniture, only a four-legged wooden table, a solitary wood chair to go with it, and a battered couch resting in front of the empty stone fireplace.

He must have used the couch to sleep, Wes thought, spying a rolled wool blanket and two pillows. A thin layer of dust coated the silent room, likely proof that his missing uncle hadn't been back to this remote refuge in recent months.

But there was this: a reel-to-reel tape recorder sitting on the flat wood table with a short stack of notebooks piled haphazardly nearby. The tape recorder was large and shaped like a box. The reels contained a full spool of tape, enough to capture hours of audio. A small, hand-held microphone was attached to the recorder, its slim cord loose.

Wes hovered above the table's well-worn chair, gingerly brushing away some grime with a hand before taking a seat. The tape recorder was plugged into a wall outlet, its power cable hanging over the table's edge. He turned the dial to *PLAY*. He listened as the reels began to slowly turn, a faint crackling noise soon quelled by the smooth, authoritative voice of the cabin's owner, Uncle Gordon.

I've returned from my year-long sojourn among the Munggua *people. This formerly uncontacted tribe has endured as part of a fascinating, nearly pre-Neolithic culture found only on the island's western portion. Their numbers are few, but the* Munggua *have held out in the unexplored jungles for many, many generations, perhaps since the earliest human habitation.*

Within such an expansive area, the Munggua *persisted in isolation until these past few years, making their ways unknown to outsiders. The* Munggua *even seemed to have believed they were the only people in existence, occupying a world all their own. My command of the native languages of these islands and my offering of gifts allowed me to live with these people and learn some of their most closely held secrets.*

Turning the recorder's dial to *STOP*, Wes began sorting through the piled notebooks on the table. Their pages were torn in places and sometimes heavily stained, as if Uncle Gordon had been writing while out in the field as he observed the practices of the *Munggua*. He randomly opened one of the notebooks and began to read a cursive, hand-written entry:

The necessary extract for the ritual is derived from several indigenous plants found in the jungles surrounding our village. Each inflorescent plant is poisonous in a large enough dose but, when measured and then mixed, the effect is that of a neuroleptic instead.

The subject of the ritual must consume this substance from the shaman guide's bowl approximately one hour before its commencement. Otherwise, the shock will kill the subject before the final transformation is accomplished.

Wes closed the laboratory-style notebook and examined its cover. A date range was jotted on adhesive tape near the cover's top, but nothing indicated its contents.

There were ten notebooks, each detailing about a month's worth of entries. Wes decided it would be easier to listen to the tape recordings and then peruse the notebooks later. Perhaps his uncle had left some clue about his current whereabouts near the end of his tapes. Wes' first year of medical school was over, and he now had a several-month break to delve into this mystery.

The sun shone brightly as Wes stood on the cabin's threshold and scrutinized the limber pine woods around him, the midday light sharply contrasting with the murky gloom within the cabin's four walls. He lit a cigarette and walked along the dirt trail leading up from the narrow combe where the cabin was nestled to a ridge above the valley.

Wes had hiked miles from the tertiary road where he had parked his rented truck to reach this spot. The forested valley was so secluded that no other homes were anywhere near it, the cabin idling in complete solitude. The previous owners had built the rustic abode as a hunting lodge of sorts.

Only he and Uncle Gordon knew about this place; Wes' father (Uncle Gordon's brother) was unaware it even existed. Before leaving on this last sabbatical to the islands, his uncle had bought the small property for cash. He had visited only once, living far away otherwise. Along with its deed, Uncle Gordon had included simple directions to the cabin, hiding both documents in a steel box in Wes' basement.

Why the secrecy? Uncle Gordon had told Wes he was the only one he could trust with the box. He'd hoped that Wes would take over his studies one day, delving into the mysteries of the world's primitive peoples. He also seemed to hint that something important might be left for Wes at the cabin someday. What Uncle Gordon had intended to accomplish with this place was still unclear, its purpose elusive to his nephew. But he wanted to keep the secret.

Wes looked out over a panorama of hills and valleys as he stood atop the ridge, stark white snow still cresting distant summits even in the early summer. He finished his cigarette and tossed the butt onto the ground, taking a deep breath of the cool mountain air. Wes remembered when his uncle had first disappeared, near the end of that exploratory field leave he'd taken from his research position, and how Wes' father, Craig, had done his best to help the police and Uncle Gordon's university with the open investigation.

"We've looked everywhere in this apartment," Craig said as he put another manila folder on the kitchen table, adding to the stack already there. "The police came up empty-handed, so we're wasting our time. I fear Gordon may really be the victim of foul play."

Craig seemed pained and then continued after a sigh of tired exasperation. "My brother maintained fastidious records of his personal affairs, Wes. There's nothing Gordon might have kept here that Detective Becker could use in a missing persons case. We just have Gordon's financial papers, some legal documents, and..."

"What's this?" Wes interrupted, having opened the last folder taken from Uncle Gordon's home office by Craig. He then held up a medical form filled out with a typewriter. "This looks like a recent diagnosis from Uncle Gordon's physician," Wes clarified, now seemingly intrigued. "But I'm not sure what it's about."

"Please let me see it," Craig requested, now standing over Wes, who was seated on a kitchen chair. His father quickly skimmed the form and then turned it over to read its back. "Hmmm," Craig murmured, scratching his temple for a moment. "I found this folder under some loose papers at the bottom of a desk drawer. The police must've missed this.

"It's a diagnosis for malignant glioma, a cancerous brain tumor," he finally announced, surprised. "And this is from a neurologist, not Gordon's regular doctor. There's also a recommendation for treatment and surgery following the diagnosis."

"Then Uncle Gordon could have been dying?" Wes asked urgently, realizing they may have found a genuine clue as to what had happened to his uncle.

"Yes, almost certainly," replied Craig as he read back over the form in his hands. "Even with the tumor's removal, the survival rate for glioblastoma is low. Gordon had a few more years at most. I'll have to show this to Detective Becker tomorrow."

Wes paused, uneasy, before asking another question. "He may have taken his own life instead of wasting away from cancer." Wes doubted this even as he said it; Uncle Gordon was a stalwart fighter if ever there was one. He would have never resignedly accepted his death from a disease. The man loved life more than anyone Wes had ever known.

"He could have, but where's the body? Something should have been found by now," Craig offered in response. "The passenger manifest recorded that he was on his return flight, but there's no trace of him after that. It's as if he vanished into thin air without so much as a parting goodbye."

"There's also no record here of a follow-up with the neurologist after his initial diagnosis," Wes indicated as he closed Uncle Gordon's medical records, putting the folder with its remaining papers on the stack.

"He just left for his sabbatical without any further treatment, it seems. Odd that he wouldn't have tried to buy more time with surgery."

"True," Craig agreed, his voice becoming quiet; he seemed to be holding something back from Wes. "But, if he just wanted to die alone, why would he come back home? He didn't see any of us after his return. If he was planning an anonymous suicide, why not do it out on that faraway island, where no one would ever find the body?"

Wes rested at the table with the tape recorder, deciding not to smoke while in the cabin. He was worried cigarette smoke might somehow damage his uncle's tapes, and the air in the cabin was already quite noisome without tobacco fumes being added in.

Uncle Gordon had been very much alive after his plane trip home, Wes thought. He had returned to this cabin and chronicled his stay among the *Munggua* for some archival purpose. But how had Uncle Gordon arrived here (Wes hadn't seen a vehicle beside the only accessible road for many miles) and what had happened after these tapes were recorded?

He pressed *PLAY* again and the tape reels turned, Uncle Gordon's voice assuming a relaxed, narrational tone:

I have spent considerable time in other parts of this archipelago. However, the magnificent vastness of the western island's lush tropical boscage still takes my breath away. When viewed from the high hills not far from my hosts' village, the jungle canopy seems to have no end. The Munggua *people live in a kind of untouched paradise, bountiful, where everything they could desire is within their reach. Even post-contact, the* Munggua *remain fiercely protective of their privacy and native autonomy.*

Their connection to the land is a profound one and informs their spiritual views. Reality to them is the flowering sago tree; the blue ocean; a turbulent, unchecked river; and the almost immeasurable, trackless mangrove swamp—these were the whole universe to the Munggua *until strangers intruded upon their way of life.*

The Munggua *believe that spirits inhabit all things, even their bodily extremities. Certain spirits live in a man's fingers or nose, for example, and can cause mischief if offended or otherwise provoked. The* Munggua *also contend the spirits of their ancestors live on and watch over them, granting immense power that can be possessed through intricate ceremony and ritual sacrifice.*

Herein lies my interest in these fervent, often pitiless people: tribes I encountered on the island farther south during previous expeditions relayed tales of folk who could metamorphize a man into a giant worm, the resultant worm form attaining nigh-immortality, even near godhood.

The name of this ritual of metamorphosis can be translated as "the Boneless King," referring to the worm's status as an invertebrate. It was this tribe's most sacred rite, and they considered it proof of their mastery over nature and the spiritual world.

The tribesmen who related this fable to me insisted it was true despite the apparently fantastical elements. They then said the tribe who practiced this rite lived on the same island and were reputed to be flesh eaters. The tribe was greatly feared and its members were left to themselves, having headhunted their neighbors to extinction in the distant past.

When the Munggua *were first discovered by Westerners, the description of their territory and the peoples' characteristics matched that of the "Boneless King" tales told to me by the island's local tribes. Given my condition, I knew that I must seek out the* Munggua *and learn the secret of their ritual. I had a rapport with the island people and there was nothing left for me other than to pursue this chance to cheat death.*

Uncle Gordon's narrative was cut short as Wes again put the recorder's dial to *STOP*. He rummaged through his duffel bag, which he had left near the cabin's tiny kitchenette, and finally removed a large brown envelope.

Wes slid from the envelope a black and white photograph, examining it closely. The photo was of Dr. Gordon Klingler, taken some years ago during his first journey to the islands.

Square-jawed and confident, Uncle Gordon stood at the center of a cluster of natives grasping spears. The men were grim-faced, as if enduring some unwanted intrusion. Uncle Gordon appeared oblivious to the men's demeanor, smiling broadly at the camera in his jungle attire, his shirt sleeves rolled up to his forearms.

Putting the photo back, Wes searched the cabinets above the kitchenette's sink. He found two cans of corned beef hash and opened them with an opener he found next to them. *Uncle Gordon didn't leave much food*, Wes thought, disappointed. *I'm glad I brought some of my own.*

One of the electric stove's burners glowed orange, a covered steel pot resting atop it. Wes drank thirstily from the sink faucet, hands cupped as there were no drinking glasses. The rusted, iron-mineral taste of the well water was disagreeable. He could faintly detect the whirring of a generator, the sound coming from somewhere below the cabin's floorboards.

He also left the generator running—a fire hazard, Wes considered, mildly concerned. *He must have, or I wouldn't have been able to run the tapes or use the stove. I wonder how much fuel I have left? I'll have to check later.*

Wes spooned the warmed hash onto a plate and went outside for lunch. He sat on some level rocks piled next to a thicket of trees and ate his simple meal in the afternoon sun. The old generator's whirring could be heard from outside as he was sitting close to the cabin; he heard it intermittently falter with a sputter.

Heading back inside, Wes pressed *PLAY* again and sat at the table. Uncle Gordon's voice now sounded vaguely anxious.

So, for months, I lived with the Munggua. *They shared their rich oral tradition with me, celebrating and venerating their ancestors, who they believe are still with them. As the* Munggua *and related island people have no written language, all their collective science, religion, history, and cosmology is passed on through storytelling, generation after generation.*

I've transcribed much of their language in my notebooks, finding it very similar to many native dialects on the islands but with some remarkable distinctions. After some months, I felt I had gained these people's confidence. The Munggua *seemed to see in me a kindred soul despite my outsider's appearance.*

Then, one night, the Munggua *head man—his name is Kolokam—told me a new story, one I hadn't heard from any other villagers before or subsequently. This story may be the tribe's oldest and, while not exactly a creation myth, it certainly includes the origin of the* Munggua *as a people.*

In this story, a man called Gimi wanders alone for what seems like an eternity, moving from place to place, until he comes upon an uninhabited forest that will one day become the heart of the Munggua*'s tribal lands. Spent from his long travels, he falls to the ground under the sprawling jungle's tightly entwined cover, sinking into a deep and interminable sleep.*

Around Gimi's head, limbs, and bodily trunk, the tangled underbrush's porous soil begins to claim him as he slumbers, restful and unaware. He is drawn down into the soupy, terrestrial detritus of the jungle floor, changing and reforming into a colossal, man-sized worm within this thin layer of earth.

More people come to this place and, eventually, Gimi becomes their king and is worshipped by them as a deity of the forest and the land. He protects his people and watches over them, elevating worthy elders to become "Boneless Kings," a kind of sainthood among the Munggua. *In the ground under their sacred place, these ancestors are ensconced, dormant in prolonged estivation but still heedful and aware.*

This is the legend! This is why I came to the Munggua; *so that I could learn this ritual of "the Boneless King," apparently as real as I had hoped.*

I questioned Kolokam, asking if he had ever seen an elder transformed into one of the revered guardian worms. Reluctant at first, he then said that he had and that it had been an incredible sight to behold.

I asked if I could witness the ritual and whether an elder had been chosen or soon would be. Kolokam was silent. He then slowly said one had been chosen and that he would be the spirit guide to lead the transformation.

The Munggua *had intended that I would leave them before the ritual, but Kolokam told me I could view it if I so desired. The ritual would be held on the night of the new moon, in the thick of the jungle outside the village.*

The night of the new moon came. I was led to a secluded spot, perhaps a mile from where the Munggua *maintained their settlement of thatched huts and flimsy rattan enclosures. A village man said they had kept this place in the jungle hidden from me until they felt I could be fully trusted. Now, I was to see their most secretive and closely held rite take place.*

I stood at the edge of a jungle clearing, perhaps with as many as a dozen other men within view. Upright wooden poles carved with the symbols of headhunting adorned the clearing's edges. From the poles hung shrunken human heads, the mouths of these unfortunates stitched tightly shut.

Standing torches were interspersed among the headhunting poles, their burning fires illuminating a bed of turned-up soil at the clearing's center. A naked man, very elderly and wizened, was guided by each arm and then lain down in the soil. The man appeared quite groggy and benumbed, as if he was thoroughly intoxicated.

The old man placed his arms over his chest and closed his eyes. Kolokam appeared from the jungle's inky shadows, festooned in a bird-feathered shaman's headdress and chalk-white face paint. A bone ornament fashioned from the tusks of a wild boar protruded from his nose and his expression was contorted into an unnerving grin.

Kolokam was now as fearsome as could be imagined. He let out a savage howl as he stood above the supine elder. His ceremonial stave was held aloft, its raw wood twisted into the shape of a writhing flatworm.

The other men from the village drummed and sang and danced, Kolokam chanting a refrain as they shrieked and ululated. They leaped from one side of the clearing to the other and gyrated frantically, a coarse sweat drenching their nearly bare bodies.

With their mouths hanging open, the men's eyes lolled back in their heads, the spirits of this dark place having seized them and taken possession of their souls. I felt as if I was peering through a window into the distant past, glimpsing a primeval spectacle that might have been found at the dawn of man's antiquity.

As this enthralling display progressed, the elder suddenly began to stir, his body at first showing only a tremor but then falling into spastic convulsions. A man, a prisoner, was brought forth and tied to one of the headhunting poles. Kolokam would later tell me that the man had murdered his brother and that this was his punishment: to be consumed in an act of sacrificial cannibalism.

The elder's body bulged horrifically, his skin taking on a slick, jet-black sheen. His limbs and torso swelled enormously before collapsing into the shape of a monstrous dark brown worm, the pointed head long and snout-like.

The worm slithered toward the man lashed to the pole. The man tried to scream but his tongue had been cut out. His eyes protruded in terror as the worm engulfed his lower half, a glistening secretion beginning to dissolve his appendages.

I was both fascinated and repulsed by what was happening. The man soon went limp, the remainder of his carcass eventually disappearing into the smothering folds of the giant worm. Satiated, the worm burrowed into the soil where only moments before its human form had commenced the ritual, taking its place in the earth among the Munggua*'s forefathers.*

The sun had almost set, and the cabin was dimly lit from the outside. Wes put the recorder's dial to *STOP* when he finally noticed that evening had come. The jarring tale on Uncle Gordon's tapes had made him forget where he was and what was around him.

A single light bulb dangled from the cabin's panel ceiling, unshielded and unlit. Wes stood to pull the lightbulb's cord and bright light filled the cabin's middle interior, leaving the table and chair where he had sat still in shadows.

Wes took a cigarette from a pack in his duffel bag and opened the cabin's front door. The air outside was cool, but the evening was warmer than the last. Soon, these mountains would bask in the summer heat, as they always did.

Lighting his cigarette, Wes inhaled its flavor, taking in a long draw through the cigarette's filter. He stared into the cabin from where he sat on a tree stump, the door propped open, light from the cabin ceiling's lightbulb spilling out into the surrounding night.

Wes recalled that, when his father had dropped him off at home after searching Uncle Gordon's off-campus apartment, he had told

Wes something odd, even disturbing. Wes supposed it might have come from the apprehension that Wes had sensed in his father when they'd discussed Uncle Gordon's speculative murder or suicide.

Its wide bumper coming close to the sidewalk facing Wes' modest one-story bungalow, Craig parked his convertible, Wes beside him in the passenger seat. Craig hoped Wes would be able to afford something better after medical school—that he might even purchase his first home if he wed after graduating. But Wes was still single as far as he knew; he was tight-lipped about girls, as always.

"Well, here we are," Craig announced, watching his son push open the car door from the front seat. "I'll tell you what Detective Becker says after we speak on Monday."

Wes paused on the edge of his car seat and turned to look at his father. "Do you really think your brother would take his own life?" Wes asked emphatically, raising his voice. "That would be so unlike Uncle Gordon. I can't believe he'd ever do it."

"Neither do I, really," Craig replied, looking away from Wes onto the empty street, his expression preoccupied. "That's why I first suggested he was murdered. Years ago, Gordon confided something to me that I still think about."

"Like he was going to disappear someday? Something like that?" Wes tensed, silently pleading with his father to not share something even worse.

"No," Craig answered. "He said that he would find a way to live forever, that he'd discover the secret of eternal life. Really. Gordon was entirely serious. He said this after his maiden voyage to the islands, quite a few years ago. Seems very strange now, especially after his disappearance. I don't know what to make of it."

Closing the cabin door behind him, Wes sat on the table's chair and pressed *PLAY*. Uncle Gordon resumed his account of the *Munggua* and their customs.

There have been small signs of my growing weakness since I've been on the island. Dizziness, as well as some nausea—I even almost vomited once or twice. I haven't let Kolokam or the rest of the Munggua *know that I am dying. If I did, they likely would have never allowed me to participate in the ritual, even as a trusted observer. My reasons for wanting to see the rite of "the Boneless King" would have been all too transparent.*

In bits and pieces, Kolokam revealed to me just what is in the neuroleptic extract used in the ritual. I've recorded this information in my field notes. Interestingly, Kolokam stated that all that's necessary for the transformation is the botanical extract and the soil of the sacred grove, so infused with mystical potency is the earth there from millennia of ancestor worms resting under the dirt. The ritual chanting and cavorting are entirely for show, done to reaffirm the Munggua*'s religious traditions.*

And a sacrifice. The sacrifice of a prisoner is effective, but the ritual's success is almost guaranteed if a close family member is used in a prisoner's place. That the chosen relation voluntarily comes to the place of sacrifice is an absolute requirement.

The worm form can be achieved with only the first two components of the ritual. Still, the new worm can only become forever undying with the sacrifice of a human life. A life for a life eternal.

I plan on digging in the sacred grove late at night while the village sleeps, obtaining enough soil to...

Without warning, the light went out in the cabin and the tape recording stopped as if the power had been abruptly cut off. Surprised, Wes stumbled from his seat and groped his way to his duffel bag, finding the camping flashlight he had brought for the trip. He flipped the flashlight's top switch on and a wide beam shone onto the cabin floor, allowing him to see again.

I need to find the trapdoor to the cellar; it's got to be in a corner somewhere, Wes reasoned, probing around the room with his light. *The generator's down there. Maybe it finally ran out of fuel.*

A dusty floor mat was in a corner past the couch where Uncle Gordon had set up his improvised bed. Wes turned over the mat with a foot, exposing a trapdoor with a handle. The hatch didn't seem to be locked.

Resting the flashlight on top of the tarp mat's turned-up leaf, Wes grabbed the hatch's iron ring and pulled, opening the trapdoor onto a set of short wooden stairs. Flashlight in hand, Wes crept down the steps into the darkness below.

The earthen cellar smelled of wet soil and gasoline, its underground atmosphere likely as stale as the cabin's air when he had arrived this morning. Crouching slightly beneath the low ceiling, Wes shined his flashlight along the cellar's walls, spying the idle generator near its back. He began to step forward in search of any fuel canisters he might use.

The ground beneath him was spongy as he approached, gleaming under the beam of his flashlight, seemingly saturated with a fine coating of slime. His foot then sank, involuntarily caught on something.

A glinting, pointed tail whipped from the moistened dirt, wrapping itself around Wes' legs and contorting around his waist and belly. He gasped in utter panic, falling back only to be enveloped by the humongous worm's fleshy interior lobes, digestive fluids dousing him.

One of Wes' arms was pulled into the worm's spiraling folds, corrosive mucus burning his skin. Wes cried out and struggled feebly, his remaining arm quickly consumed and then finally his head, overwhelmed by the turning and undulating of the worm's massive body.

The invertebrate worm form of Uncle Gordon lay in the hallowed soil of the *Munggua*, having achieved its primordial deification. It once again submerged itself in the earthen cellar floor, lying in wait for the warmer days ahead.

The Underworld

The young shepherd held his torch high and peered expectantly into the surrounding darkness. He thought he'd heard a noise somewhere in the distance, but now only the deathly silence of the night greeted him. *What was that?* Costa thought, now alarmed. It had seemed like the cry of some animal, but he couldn't be certain.

He turned and slowly walked away from the cliff's sloping ledge. Ahead stretched the subtle trail of footprints left by his father and the hunting party, leading deep into the cave. The band of men had tracked the wolves for several days to what they believed was their lair, but this cave seemed to be something else. What was once a natural cavern had been recast into a kind of hypogeum, with ghastly totems of carnage set on either side of its entrance. *Who could have put such a warning here? Surely not the wolves,* Costa thought as he scrutinized the totems, shivering slightly in the cool nighttime air.

There were sudden cries, as if the men had been startled, their astonished gasps echoing from the cavern below. Costa heard his father as he strode forward to investigate: "Costa, remain on your guard!" A pause. Then: "It's nothing, only a picture on the wall."

Obeying his father without a word, Costa climbed back to the dusty, flat plateau that met the cave's mouth and resumed his watch. He made a final glance at the entrance totems. They were fashioned from human skulls, any flesh long since stripped bare. Shuddering involuntarily, Costa again gazed out into the hushed night and the stark wilderness around him, its mass of tortured oaks and twisted brambles abutting the foot of the cave's barren hill.

Now that he was sure his son was at his station, Rufus returned his attention to the strange mural. Under the light of their torches, he and the other shepherds studied the daubed ochre rendering of a she-wolf suckling her two cubs. The painting was large, sprawling across the wall of the cave. What had shocked Rufus and his men was the strikingly lifelike depiction of the mural's cubs, portrayed as a disturbing mélange of wolf and human child, their eyes feral but keen, their paws almost like hands.

"There is much more to this wolf-pack than we suspected," Rufus said, fear creeping into his voice as he looked over the grim faces at his side. "These are not ordinary wolves, but profane spirits, cursed by the gods for some terrible crime. Stephanus spoke the truth when he said these beasts can assume the form of men."

Stepping away from the wall painting, Rufus pointed onward. "We must be quick. Aurelia may be somewhere in the cave."

The party followed Rufus deeper into the tenebrous passageway, making fleeting glances at the mural as they filed past. As they descended into depths of the cavern, the band's waning torches cast gigantic shadows, exaggerated imitations of the cave's hanging stalactites, protruding rock formations, and the men's own proportions.

From among the villagers Rufus had chosen four men and his elder son for his hunting party. Their steadings had been beset by a pack of roaming wolves and, while the attacks had lasted less than a fortnight, the loss of livestock was all but unbearable. Their village was isolated from the larger towns and cities; the provincial authorities in the distant capital were too far removed to be reached in time. The final attack ended with one shepherd's daughter being carried off by the wolves, taken from her bed as she slept.

Aurelia's father, Caius, unexpectedly halted, stopping the party in its tracks. "Did you hear that?" he said to his fellows, his voice strained and urgent as he choked out the words. "There's a girl sobbing, somewhere ahead. That's my daughter. My Aurelia!"

The men listened, but all that was audible was the distant sound of dripping water monotonously tapping against stone. In a panic, Caius pushed past Rufus and another shepherd, rushing forward into the darkness of the cave, his torch held out before him. Caius fell with a clatter and disappeared, crying out as the light from his torch was abruptly extinguished.

Shouting down into the cave's passage, Rufus exclaimed, "Caius, you fool, you've put us all in danger!" He then scoured the blackness with his torch but failed to see where Caius had fallen. Rufus turned to his men, hastily instructing them: "Go grab him, and then let's search for any sign of Aurelia. Caius couldn't have gotten too far ahead."

Rufus had only taken a few steps before he noticed two sets of glowing red eyes watching the men intently from the cave's gloaming recesses. Under flickering torchlight, the faint outline of an enormous wolf's head appeared, with a second wolf of similar size trailing not far behind it.

The first wolf leaped as Rufus drew his *gladius* from his belt, a relic from his time in the legion. The shepherd before Rufus was taken down with a piercing scream, the massive wolf tearing the man's throat out with one quick laceration from its jaws. Rufus spun, finding several more sets of glinting lupine eyes propagating around him in the shadows.

Rufus thrust with his *gladius*, stabbing deeply into a charging wolf. Howling, the beast fell aside. Rufus dropped his sputtering torch and bolted past its bleeding carcass. Two wolves gave chase, but Rufus's aged yet sturdy legs sped him forward. The dying shrieks of his men rang out from the cavern walls as they were torn to gory shreds, the victims of yet more wolves.

Tumbling out onto the hill's rocky plateau, Rufus nearly stumbled over the mutilated body of his son, the boy's dead eyes staring up into the night's starry heavens. The wolves continued to pursue their quarry, loping down through the brush surrounding the sloping hill and then out into the open fields spanning it, the waving grasses trampled beneath Rufus's sandaled feet.

As he ran, Rufus rapidly scanned the moonlit horizon for somewhere to climb, anywhere the wolves might not reach him. Not far ahead was a hillside cluster of sparsely distributed trees near an outcropping of jutting rocks.

Scaling the trunk of a sagging oak, Rufus pulled himself onto its generous bough and lay, arms clutching the wide branch. He crawled along its length, reaching a spot at its middle, near the craggy cliffs of the hill. Rufus checked his belt and realized he had dropped his *gladius* as he'd fled the caves.

The howls of the wolf pack grew nearer as they closed in on his hillside hiding place. Out the corner of his eye, Rufus spied the shape of a huge wolf perched on a cliff facing his tree branch. The wolf pounced just as Rufus tried to roll away, ripping him from the branches of the oak and onto the ground below. Rufus was silent as he met his death in the slavering jaws of the black wolf, a stoic soldier until the end.

Dragging the mangled corpse of the hunting party's leader behind it, the black-furred wolf returned to its pack. The alpha dropped Rufus's savaged remains onto the cave floor, where it lay surrounded by the gnawed and littered bones of the wolf pack's prey, both man and animal.

The wolf stretched out onto its forepaws before its assembled pack-mates, almost fluidly metamorphosing into a man. A teenage girl sat before a great gray wolf crouching on its haunches, her plain linen tunic torn and disheveled as she looked on.

The man rose from the cave floor and brought the girl to her bare feet, wrapping her in his sinewy arms in a perverse embrace. At first caressing the girl's neck, his bloody hand came to rest upon her shoulder as he began to speak to his brethren: "Soon, there will be new cubs," the man said, his voice a low and menacing growl. "The pack will swell in number. The usurpers will then know fear, as did our forebearers who were laid to waste before them."

Wild-eyed and filthy, the girl tittered insanely as the pack leader finished his vow, her mind mostly gone. The man turned her to face him, leaning down to meet the girl's parched lips and kissing her deeply on the mouth. The wolf pack howled in unison, a chilling howl of vengeance, their call reverberating off the blood-drenched walls of the wolf den and echoing out into the desolate night.

***

Appius and Lucius sat idly beside each other on a bench in the provincial governor's villa, one of many carved marble benches in the lengthy hallway. They rested in the shade of the villa's columnated front entrance, finding their seat cool to the touch despite the hot day outside.

Stirring for a moment, Lucius peered down the empty hallway. At the end of the row of benches was a statue of the emperor in military dress, the unoccupied space's only guardian. At once both regal and ascendant, the emperor's likeness conveyed a spirit of triumph after many hard-won victories. His uncle, Lucius noticed, was nodding off, but started when a young attendant appeared at his side.

"This way, please. The proconsul will see you now," the attendant said stiffly, walking quickly ahead and not bothering to note whether he was being followed. The travel-weary twosome trudged after the youth, who soon stopped in front of an open archway. "Here. Someone will return for you after your meeting with the proconsul." Unsmiling, the attendant then strode off, failing to make eye contact with either of his charges even once.

Appius glanced over at his nephew as they stood before the archway. "Big city manners," he said, shrugging wryly. Then, gesturing forward, he said, "You lead the way, Lucius. Proconsul Drusus hasn't seen you since you were a child."

Lucius stepped into the proconsul's official chambers, an open, spacious office featuring shelf after shelf of bound scrolls along its brightly painted walls. The arched and glassless windows of the chamber provided a picturesque view of the capital's calm seaside harbor and the azure summer sky under which it was sheltered. A stern-looking older man, robed in the long tunic and *pallium* of his position, turned to greet the visitors as Lucius drew near, Appius at his side.

"So, this is Rufus Norbanus' younger son, Lucius," the man said, at first seeming dispassionate but then breaking into a broad smile, the creases around his eyes stretching to his graying temples. "Come," the proconsul said as he looked over Lucius, "sit here and let's catch up on what the family has been doing out on the estates."

Proconsul Publius Claudius Drusus embraced Appius by clasping both the man's muscular forearms before resting on a reclining couch near his desk, offering the remaining two seats to Appius and Lucius.

"I'm afraid I am the bearer of bad news, Publius Drusus," Appius explained, somber as he braced himself for what was to come. "My brother, Rufus Flaccus, is dead, as is his elder son and my nephew, Costa. They were slain in the pursuit of a girl from our village who had been taken by a pack of wolves. None in the hunting party had returned after more than a week, so we have assumed the worst." Appius studied Publius Drusus's austere, aquiline face, worried that even Rufus's former commander might be shattered after learning about the death of his old friend.

Publius sat in silence as Rufus finished speaking. "Are you sure, Appius?" he said slowly, stunned. "You have nothing but a prolonged absence to confirm their deaths?" Publius had become visibly crestfallen, an abrupt change from his almost buoyant demeanor just moments ago.

"The council of elders debated sending a rescue party, but the howls of the wolves were heard outside the village soon after," Appius replied, feeling a slight chill upon recalling that night's rapacious howling. "If Rufus and his men had found the wolf den, either they would have slain the wolves, or the wolves killed them. The hunter, Quintus, was with the party and he could track a beast to the ends of the world. They surely found what they were looking for."

Publius stood and walked to an open window, his hands meeting behind his back. Gazing out past the sheer cliffs at the villa's periphery, he said, "So that is why you are here? To ask for my intervention?"

Appius arose from his seat. "Yes, Proconsul, we ask that you send a *centuria* from your garrison to deal with these predators once and for all. We request Marcus Arcturus as the centurion, a good friend of both Rufus Flaccus and myself." Appius uttered these words directly and firmly, knowing this was likely the only chance he and his people had to save themselves.

"So many men, Appius! How could you need that many legionaries?" Publius said as he turned to face Appius, his face betraying his sadness and incredulity.

Having said almost nothing during the conversation, Lucius suddenly interrupted, his voice taut and urgent: "These are not just wolves, Proconsul Drusus. These are the malign spirits of the dead who have come upon us, driven by a vendetta against the living. My belief is that they are the *Etruscī*, returned to despoil the lands taken from them by our ancestors. But they are yet flesh and blood and can be returned to the netherworld with a sword."

Publius' heavy brow furrowed, his face now appearing almost angry instead of despondent. "Those tales of the *Etruscī* are nothing but superstition, stories to frighten unruly children," he said, the scornful annoyance in his tone evident as he waved his hand. "Wolves have preyed upon the province's herds for generations, but they are just that: wolves. Merely common beasts impelled by the need to eat and to survive." Publius turned to Appius as if for support, but was met instead by morose silence.

"I beg your pardon, Proconsul," Lucius said at last. "We have as witness one of the most trusted men in our village. He swore these wolves can walk on two legs after taking the shape of men. What he saw one night nearly sent him to Orcus." Lucius breathed in and then gulped before continuing, halfway stricken by fear as he began to retell Stephanus' story.

"Stephanus, the village cartwright and a respected elder, was on his smallholding after the attacks first began. He was outside securing his shed against the depredations of the wolves; valuables had been found missing from the village after the attacks. How mere wolves could steal coin and belongings wasn't clear, but it soon became so.

"As Stephanus barred the shed door, he spied the silhouettes of several wolves in the moonlight. They began prowling up the path to his family's villa. Stephanus stopped and hid behind the shed, not wanting to draw their attention. His wife and children had left to stay with his wife's sister in a neighboring village the day before, so the house was now unoccupied.

"Once the wolf pack reached the entrance, they began to transform, shifting and taking on new shapes. Without so much as a sound, the strange beasts assumed human form and stood upright, unclothed and unshorn. The bare, shaggy men then forced open the villa's front door, breaking the lock with only their brute strength.

"The bandits piled in and soon emerged holding a bulging sack, which was then strapped to the backs of one of the men. The house thieves fell to their knees and regained the bodies of monstrous wolves, metamorphosing in mere moments. The pack gathered and let out a blood-curdling victory howl before disappearing into the night, the clanging of Stephanus's stolen silverware ringing behind them as they fled."

Lucius paused his narrative and eyed Publius' face, but the older man gave nothing away. "Well, Stephanus was petrified in his hiding place, trembling in terror, now certain our little community had somehow brought the fury of the gods down upon us. He prayed to Lupercus that what he had seen was only a trick of a frightened mind, but in his heart he knew otherwise."

Publius studied Lucius for a moment and then moved to seat himself behind his desk. Speaking forthrightly to both men, Publius said, "I will make an offering at the temple to Apollo this evening and let the divinity speak to me through the sibyl. You will have my answer in the morning once I have pondered the sibyl's riddle. An attendant will now show you to your rooms."

Indicating an end to their meeting, Publius Drusus stood once again and turned to look out the window at the midday sun reflecting off the sparkling waters of the harbor. Appius and Lucius stepped into the hallway, finding a second attendant waiting for them. They were led across the villa's sprawling courtyard, itself lined with shrubbery and marble statuary and with a flowing fountain at its center. The attendant paused at a suite of rooms facing the courtyard and opened its door for the guests.

"So, this is where they put our satchels," Appius observed as he reached down to search their luggage. "I was worried someone had run off with them."

"What do you think?" Lucius said, an authentic bewilderment hanging over him as he sat on his mattress and watched Appius unpack. "Will Proconsul Drusus help us?"

"I believe so," Appius assured him, digging through a small leather *loculus* as he spoke. "Publius' belief in the gods is not strong, but he may listen to the oracle. My own opinion is that Publius may just be looking for a scapegoat, pinning the decision to deploy troops to the outlands on the sibyl's prattle instead of on himself."

"You don't believe in the gods, do you, Appius?" Lucius seemed almost surprised as he asked the question to his uncle.

"I believe in our family, our village, and our safety, Lucius," Appius replied matter-of-factly. "My brother and my nephew are dead, as are several other villagers. If Publius must burn some incense or 'sacrifice' nine *popona* to save us from the wolves then so be it."

"I'm going to visit the villa baths before the *cena*," Lucius said, quickly burying the subject at hand. "I'm dusty after our long journey. I just hope Proconsul Drusus didn't notice."

Lucius left the guest rooms to walk to the baths, excited to indulge in such a modern convenience. He thought back to their meeting with

Publius Drusus and how the proconsul had seemed almost afraid to admit the wolves might be the vengeful spirits of the *Etruscī*.

Publius Drusus, Appius, his own father, and Marcus Arcturus had all served together in the legion, stationed at what was then the far-flung edge of the Empire. *Is there something about the wolves Appius and Publius Drusus know but are not admitting?* Lucius mused as he entered the villa's *caldarium*, the heated room's hot, moist air quickly opening the pores of his dry skin. Lucius sat to remove his worn sandals and then quietly prayed, hoping his father's old friend would send aid before it was too late.

***

The late afternoon sun bore down on Appius and Lucius' horse-drawn cart as it entered the village's main thoroughfare, the men exhausted after their days-long journey. The villagers had been roused by the loud clacking of iron-shod wheels over the westerly hills and emerged from their simple dwellings along the wide road to watch the travelers' return.

An older man followed by a great, heavily-jowled dog opened the door to his home and approached the cart as it slowly rolled past. The dog accompanying the man bore fresh scars across its nose and cheek, evidence of the most recent wolf attack.

"*Salvē*, Appius Flaccus. Do you bring good news or bad news back with you? I pray your time with the proconsul was not wasted."

Appius drew the cart to a gradual stop, and the man reached up to put a brawny hand on his shoulder before Appius could even answer him.

"A full *centuria* will arrive in less than half a fortnight, Atticus," Appius announced, with no small measure of enthusiasm despite his weariness. "And Marcus Arcturus will lead them. The wolves will meet their end when they harass us again."

"Excellent, Appius!" Atticus said, patting Appius' shoulder in thanks. "The legion will deal with this menace. We must prepare a temporary barracks for the men before their arrival." Atticus then strode off to converse with the villagers who had gathered nearby, his guard dog in tow.

Appius urged his cart horse down to where the main road ended, finally branching off into the outlying farmsteads. His family's small villa was on the village outskirts, with its own plot of land—it had been bequeathed to Rufus Flaccus as payment for his services to the legion. Lucius now lived with his aunt, uncle, and their children in the villa, his father and brother gone. Lucius's mother had died years before.

Lucius removed his wide-brimmed hat, hung it up, and undid the brooch holding his drab *lacerna*. His travel clothes would be stored away after laundering, he hoped for the foreseeable future. Appius was greeted by his wife, Aelia, and his children, who told him a supper had been prepared for their coming. After supper, Lucius and Appius sat outside on wood *sella* taken from the kitchen, watching a burnt orange sun set over the hills they had just traveled.

"I explored many lands in my youth as part of the legion," Appius said, breaking an uncomfortable silence after the sun had disappeared behind the hills. "But I'm sure your father must have told you some of our stories. Publius Drusus and Marcus Arcturus were valiant men, stalwarts against the *Germani* and other barbarous adversaries. Why, I remember this one time, we—"

"Father never spoke to us about his time in the legion," Lucius said suddenly, his gaze still fixed on the now-dark horizon. "He was proud of his service, but the killing… it never sat well with him. I think he was afraid he'd become used to it." Lucius looked over at Appius, unsure whether Rufus had revealed such anxieties to his younger brother.

"Rufus never flinched. He met death head-on and spit in its face. I'm sure that's how he met his end with the wolves." Appius smiled slightly as he spoke, as if recalling some act of bravery. "He must have taken a wolf or two with him."

Lucius leaned back on his stool and rested his brow in his hand. "Father did tell us one story about his coming home after a long campaign," Lucius finally said after a lengthy pause. "He probably told it to us as the story was so peculiar. You were with him if I remember correctly."

"Aye, I might recall it. Did the story involve a woman? A woman and her two sons?"

"That's the one," Lucius confirmed. "Marcus Arcturus had allowed his men to break ranks after the long campaign and leave with their own *contubernia* instead of waiting with the rest of the legion. The discharged *contubernales* passed near the borderlands of the Empire on the way home to their families.

"Even though Father was their *decanus*, you and Father broke from the other men returning home, all of them eager to see loved ones. Off from the roadside was a thatched cottage, partially hidden by the dense woods."

Appius agreed, seeming to recall more of the story now. "That's it. A strange old woman lived in that hut, half-mad, I think. But what else did your father tell you about her?"

"That she invited you in, both of you, and bid you stay the night," Lucius replied, a moment of clarity coming upon him. "She told you her own story, one about the wolves that roamed the black forestlands. She sat you next to the fire, gave you something to eat, and then began her odd tale..."

Rufus put aside his wooden spoon and began sopping up the last remnants of gruel with a thick slice of dark bread. He and Appius had eaten only early that morning and it was now close to sunset. The compatriots were tired after their long trek across the borderlands, having made most of the journey on foot. When they had spied a lonely cottage at the woodland boundary, they immediately sought shelter within.

"Gratias tibi. *We appreciate your hospitality," Rufus said as he watched the woman and Appius eating, the three of them having dined in polite silence until that moment. The trio sat around a smoldering firepit, the fire's charcoal-colored smoke drifting up through a blackened hole in the straw roof of the cottage. "We're still a long way from our village," Rufus continued amicably. "This is what the imperial subjects in Aegyptus might call an 'oasis' along our journey home."*

"I have little company, and you men are both in the legion. Think nothing of it," the woman replied casually, finishing with her meal and setting her bowl aside. She stood and took the men's bowls and her own to a washing basin laid on the cottage's earthen floor. Rufus observed her movements as she cleaned up, guessing her weathered appearance hid her actual age. She may even have been quite beautiful at one time, not so long ago.

"You had better check your pack mule," the woman said as she washed. "It could be a long night. The forest's edge is not safe, but I live here nonetheless."

"What's your name, woman?" Appius asked abruptly, having been quiet since taking his seat by the fire. "You've invited us in for the night, but we still don't know your name."

"I am Servilia," the woman replied, almost bothered by the question. "These lands are not my native lands, and the people who dwell past this forest are not my kin."

"I am Appius Flaccus, and this is my older brother, Rufus Flaccus," Appius said, with Rufus nodding briefly as he was introduced. "Our families are waiting for us farther along, and we hope to return to them safely. Once we have slept, we'll be on our way again in the morning."

A lone wolf howled somewhere out in the forest. Servilia looked toward the crude door of the one-room cottage and then back down at the basin, as if hoping the unsettling call would go unmentioned.

"I'll go check on our mule," said Rufus. "She could use more feed grass if we sleep past sunrise." He stood and began striding toward the cottage door, wondering why their host had ignored the sound of imminent danger not so far away.

"Wait, please. Don't venture outside just yet," Servilia pleaded, holding an outstretched hand toward Rufus. "I must tell you a story first, to help you understand why I am here, alone in these woods." Servilia gestured for Rufus to sit again by the fire, its flickering light casting shadows over her creased, weather-beaten face. "My time may soon end, and I need to pass something on to you before you take your leave of me."

Appius glanced over at his brother as Rufus took his seat on one of several decrepit wooden stools placed around the firepit. Servilia then reached under her mottled tunic to produce a silver-white coin hanging from a chain around her neck. The coin shone brightly as Servilia dangled the pendant near the light of the fire, its gleaming, argent surface in sharp contrast to the cottage's colorless, dingy interior.

"This amulet was forged in Hispania," she murmured, as if dragging forward distant memories. "It has protected me in this desolate place from what lurks at night in the forest."

Servilia then closed her hand around the pendant, suddenly breaking what was almost a hypnotic moment. Rufus and Appius were now very quiet, both feeling there was much more to this beggarly woman than they had first believed.

"I met him at the festival of the Lupercalia when I was only a girl. A man appeared in the crowd wearing the mask of the wolf. He took me and loved me. Soon after, I found I was with child—twins. The children were born in secret, away from my family, as there was no father.

"I raised my two sons alone, not far from this comfortless abode I now call my home. They grew to early manhood, and that is when the bloodlust came upon them. One day, I returned home late from the market to find two wolves, distinct from each other by the color of their coats. That this had occurred was impossible, but I knew they were my sons."

Servilia stared into the fire, lost for a moment but then flaring with sudden determination. "My sons had slaughtered our small flock of sheep in their pen. They were feeding on the carcasses when I interrupted them. One appeared ready to pounce, but the other howled into the twilight, impelling both to flee. Since that day, my sons have led the wolf packs in the hills and forests of this forsaken land."

Without pausing to mark a conclusion to the story, Servilia stood and walked to the cottage wall facing the firepit, over which hung a tattered cloth. She pulled the cloth down from its hooks to display a painting, one stained into the daub itself. It was a coarse yet vivid depiction of a she-wolf suckling two cubs, her offspring demonic and half-human in appearance.

"These demi-human beasts are cursed by the gods, avatars of revenge and depraved appetites," Servilia declared as she stood before the painting, holding forth the silver pendant. "These creatures call themselves 'the

Children of Lupercus,' but they are nothing of the sort. They are infernal, and spring from the underworld itself."

Servilia stepped back toward the firepit and held the pendant before Rufus, letting it drop into his open palm. Rufus could now see the image engraved into the metal. It was much like that of the wall painting: a mother wolf with her two whelps.

"The amulet is blessed," Servilia continued vehemently, nearly shaking as she spoke, "and can seal the curse of the Luperci, trapping it in a moment of time as a moth might be cast in amber. The amulet can also act as a ward, protecting those threatened by the demons' fangs and claws."

With that, Servilia turned and let out a hacking cough, steadying herself against the wall as she did so. Facing them again, Servilia whispered, "My time is short, and they know it. The wolves close in on me. I will be too weak to use the amulet when they finally come."

Lucius turned to look at Appius in the faint moonlight, pausing the retelling of his father's story. "And then the three of you bed down to sleep, the woman's wheezing breaths soon growing shallow as she lay nearby. You and Father conspired to slip away, fearful not only that she was mad, but that she might carry the pestilence."

Stunned by the sharpness of Lucius's memory, Appius only nodded. He then said, "As we left in the dead of night, many eyes appeared outside the hut, watching us from the fringes of the forest. The wolves let us pass unmolested on the empty road, receding into the distance as we took the path home. As for what became of the woman...well. It's best not to dwell upon it."

***

"Where did you find it?" Appius asked, studying the silver pendant that swayed gently in his grasp. He recognized the relief of the she-wolf and cubs engraved into its coin.

"In a little box, among Father's personal belongings," Lucius replied, satisfied that he'd been able to recover this lost possession. "Father was very private and kept things from his days in the legion hidden away in a chest. I would have never found it if Father were still with us." More quietly, he added, "Father may have forgotten about the amulet. It might have saved him."

"That woman was mad, Lucius," Appius scoffed. "How she came upon such a fine piece of jewelry is the only unexplainable thing from her ravings. She was destitute in that shack out in the woods."

Lucius took the pendant back from Appius. "The old woman told you this amulet was blessed. By whom, I wonder?" He looped the pendant's chain around his neck and tucked its coin under his tunic.

"The priests of Lupercus, the *Luperci*? Who knows, some divinity. I believe none of it." Appius shrugged dismissively.

"Some say that Lupercus is really Faunus," Lucius noted. "The horned god of the forest. He also relishes in playing tricks on mortals, or so it is said."

"Again, nonsense. Come, let's be about it." Appius pushed open the front door to their villa and handed Lucius a heavy *pilum,* its iron point recently sharpened. Fastening his *gladius* to his belt, Appius then led Lucius down the road to the village.

It was early evening. The howling of the wolves had kept many in the village awake the previous night, and all felt better having Marcus Arcturus and the men of his *centuria* around. They had arrived that morning and were busy preparing for the return of the wolf pack.

"*Salvē*, Marcus Arcturus. Are your men ready at their stations? The wolves attacked our people in their homes when they last came upon us." Appius embraced the imposing man in centurion's uniform as they stood at the village road's center. The man's raven hair was streaked with gray, his face marred from many long campaigns.

"We await the wolves. Forty men are sequestered in your village hall and will emerge in force once the pack begins its predations. Our war hounds are with them, collared and set." Marcus Arcturus then nodded to Lucius, acknowledging the son of his best soldier and close friend.

"Excellent. Thank you, especially for sending men to family households. Four of your men are at our villa now. Should the wolves enter, they will surely be surprised." Appius smiled broadly as he said this, hopeful that the moment of revenge was at hand.

The sun began to disappear behind the hills surrounding the village. An uneasy quiet descended, as if all knew something terrible was about to happen but none dared speak of it aloud.

***

Appius and Lucius sat at the dining table with Atticus and his wife, Atticus's big dog resting at their feet.

"Your house is near the middle thoroughfare, Atticus. If the wolves come upon the road, we can rush to them and attack." Appius unconsciously put his hand over his belt as he said this, seeking the assurance his battle-worn *gladius* provided him.

A solitary wolf howl pierced the night. Distant, yes, but soon joined by a cacophony of howls much closer. Appius arose from his seat at the table just as the front door burst in violently, a sable black wolf leaping to meet his throat, the broken door falling aside.

The wolf thrashed Appius's limp body back and forth across the wooden table, blood coating the walls as Lucius reached for his *pilum*. The wolf dropped Appius from its jaws and then turned to Lucius and Atticus, finding both men armed and ready.

Baring its fangs ferociously, the wolf leaped aside as Lucius jabbed with his *pilum*. Swinging his club, Atticus was blocked by another wolf which had darted in from the village thoroughfare, the road outside now swarming with wolves of varying sizes and rustic hues.

Atticus fell under the second wolf's assault, his guard dog yowling as it was mobbed by more wolves and then brought down. Escaping through the open doorway to the road, Lucius saw what was happening: dozens, perhaps over a hundred wolves were swarming into the village, crashing against a wall of legionaries, war dogs, and armed villagers.

A soldier close to Lucius cried out as he was leaped upon by two wolves and pulled down, his *scutum* and *gladius* falling from his hands. Lucius turned and was met by an enormous auburn wolf, crouched, blood and saliva dripping from its jaws.

The wolf's great forepaws met Lucius's chest just as he reached under his tunic, knocking him back. Lucius struggled under its crushing weight, the beast's overpowering scent being almost too much to bear. With all the strength he could muster, Lucius managed to pull forth the hidden pendant with his free hand.

The pendant's coin glowed eerily with an otherworldly blue aura. The wolf recoiled and wailed, convulsing in a pantomime of excruciating pain as it fell back and then fled into the tumultuous throng around them. Recovering, Lucius pulled himself to his feet and surveyed the ongoing fray.

Bodies were strewn everywhere: some wolves, but mostly the men and dogs who had fought against them. The remaining legionaries had formed a tight circle with their *scuta* facing outward, stabbing at charging wolves attempting to break their ranks. Lucius turned and ran down the road to his family's villa, fearful his only remaining kin might also be dead.

The villa door was broken when he arrived, a bloody trail on the antechamber's floor leading away from the entrance. Lucius gripped his *pilum* with both hands and cautiously stepped into the darkened entryway. He soon found a pair of soldiers, torn and lacerated, as well as a slain wolf in the hall to the kitchen. Waves of splattered blood adorned the hallway's domestic fresco.

A low growl rumbled in the passage behind Lucius. He turned and was confronted by a sleek gray wolf a few paces away, a prominent sword gash splitting its bloodied muzzle.

The beast tensed, about to leap, just as the eerie blue light of the pendant swelled again. The wolf yelped, the sound almost pitiful, and raced away. Lucius watched it go before continuing his search. Before long, he found his aunt and the two remaining legionaries dead on the villa grounds outside.

Where are the children? Lucius thought, almost sure the wolves had taken them. His two young cousins, the daughters of Appius and Aelia, were nowhere to be seen. The villa seemed deserted now, otherwise silent save for the sounds of fighting between men and wolves, ambient in the distance. Searching further, Lucius found a torn piece of a tunic and one of the girls' loose sandals. Neither had blood on them.

The argent coin hanging from its chain glowed more brightly than ever before at this unexpected discovery, as if the pendant were attempting to lead Lucius to the girls' wolfish abductors. Lucius wandered into the night, following the faraway howling, the pendant pulling him forward.

He stumbled in the dark, the waning moon providing little illumination as he reached the low hills outside the village, trusting in pendant that shone like a floating beacon in an ocean of darkness. Soon, Lucius reached the encampment of the wolves. There, half a dozen of them lay licking their wounds around two prisoners.

The kidnapped cousins were bound and gagged, and lay resting against several sacks of stolen goods. The elder of the two girls, Norbana, saw Lucius approaching and began to struggle against her bonds, her muffled cries alerting the injured wolf pack.

Lucius strode boldly into the camp's center as the wolves arose, the pendant now blazing with a brilliant white-blue light. The wolfen creatures shrieked and howled, several limping away into the surrounding darkness, others falling and convulsing in the mud. Only one wolf, a great black beast, remained to face Lucius.

The enormous black wolf stood on its hind legs and began to reshape itself into a naked man, his ebon-hued hair matted with blood, as had been the wolf's coat. The alpha wolf, the surviving son of Servilia, reached for his blade.

"I shall kill you as a man, worthless cur," he spat, his voice harsh and venomous. "It's what one such as you deserve."

The man darted forward, slashing viciously with his curved dagger, narrowing missing Lucius's arms and throat. Lucius quickly stepped back and held the argent coin high, its unearthly bluish rays now coalescing into a loping wolf pack, translucent and ghostly in its aspect.

The celestial wolves descended from the night sky along an invisible path and thronged the man, dragging him screaming down into the earth, into the chthonian underworld of Pluto.

Lucius kept his *pilum* poised, ready for another attack, but as the moments passed in silence, he realized the daemon wolf had been cast out from this world by the noble spirits of the wolves he and his packmates had corrupted. The night on the hills was still, save for the frightened weeping of Lucius's cousins.

He reached down into the dust to pick up the pendant, having dropped it as the wolf-wraiths descended. The argent coin gleamed in the moonlight, a fresh lupine soul trapped forever within, the curse of the *Luperci* bonded with the coin's alloy.

***

"Mere years ago, all of this was but uncultivated land for a thousand paces," Lucius enthused to the slim, smartly dressed man at his side who nodded, listening intently to his host. "My laborers and I have turned this plot into a thriving olive orchard, one which sells its produce as far away as the capital. My father never thought it was possible, but we did it." Lucius leaned on the villa balcony's balustrade, smiling at the wealthy merchant.

"I remember when your town was but a village, known mostly for its rocky soil," the man remarked blithely, his tone relaxed and casual. "You're right; what you've done here is a miracle, Lucius Flaccus, blessed by the gods." The merchant then drank from his cup, looking out from the balcony at the horizon as the summer sun dipped behind the hills. It would be nighttime soon.

"Yes, blessed by the gods. As you say." Lucius suddenly seemed absent-minded, as if recollecting a past tragedy that still haunted him. Lucius then smiled again, worried his guest might notice this fleeting moment of painful distraction.

"But it grows late, Gaius Polybius," he said swiftly, pulling himself back into the present. "My wife and one of our servants will show you to your rooms. Tomorrow we will draw up the contracts and complete the sale. *Bene quiescere*."

The merchant nodded, bade Lucius goodnight, and stepped inside. Lucius turned back to peer out at the hills beyond. The marble balcony was one of his recent additions to his family's villa—an indulgence during this time of prosperity. Years had passed since the wolves had been driven from the village, the packs abruptly fleeing just as their victory over the legionaries appeared certain. They never returned.

The full moon was ripe and loomed large overhead as a warm breeze drifted over Lucius, helping to soothe his apprehension. Squinting into the darkness, Lucius thought he saw several shapes approaching from the road. They looked like animals, but he couldn't be sure.

Lucius kept the silver pendant in a ceramic urn high on a shelf in his bedroom, where his children couldn't reach it. His wife never inquired about the pendant, assuming it was some heirloom left to him by his father. Cursed, Lucius hoped the pendant would remain at the bottom of the urn for the rest of his days.

The wolves closed in, their sharp eyes shining in the dark, soon to reach the villa's front door.

Deep in the shaded urn, the pendant began to glow. The souls of the departed had returned, ready to take back their master's talisman.

Spirits of the Dead – The Third Story

Abigail stood at the door to her father's study, her breath coming in short, nervous bursts. She glanced over the ornate carvings in the door's sash, all of which depicted pastoral scenes from the English countryside.

There were images of woods and valleys, shepherds with their flocks, birds in the fields and meadows, and a hunter arching his bow. A ram's head was prominently displayed at the top of the dark mahogany door's solid frame, its curving horns projecting in relief. The rustic scenes were exceptionally detailed, and the door frame was likely older than Abigail's family's home in Wiltshire.

Abigail paused and then rapped on the study door.

"Come in," she heard her father's voice answer in reply.

She cautiously opened the door. Inside, her father was seated at his writing desk, his back to the door. She spoke in her soft child's voice: "Father, Mother said you wanted to see me."

Father turned around to face her, the light of the afternoon sun filtering through the study's partially curtained bay window. "Yes, Abigail, please come in. Come here and stand next to my desk."

Abigail did as she was told. Placed on Father's writing desk among his journals and loose papers was a bell-shaped glass display case resembling the cloches Abigail's mother used in the family garden.

Smiling pleasantly, Father said, "I have something to show you." He lifted the glass dome from its base and took a polished stone, blood-red in color, into the palm of his hand. He held out the stone in front of Abigail, as if offering it to her.

Abigail had always felt apprehension whenever she visited Father's study and personal library, which was not very often. The study was a forbidden place to the rest of the family; Arthur Barrett had always told his daughters to never enter this room without permission. Since the door to the study was nearly always kept locked, Abigail often wondered how he thought she or Evelyn would get in even if they wanted to.

Father closed his fingers tightly around the stone and then squeezed for several moments, all the while wearing a curious expression. When Father relaxed his fingers and displayed the contents of his open palm, a small grey toad rested there. The toad turned in Father's palm and gulped, but made no attempt to leap from its perch onto the study's floor.

Quickly grasping Abigail's right arm, Father deposited the live toad into her palm with his free hand. "Squeeze tightly, Abigail," he murmured. "Don't be afraid; you won't hurt him."

An impassive Abigail did as her Father asked.

"Now, open your hand and look," Father instructed.

Abigail slowly relaxed her fingers from her palm, extending them outward. The polished bloodstone from the display case was in her hand, the toad gone.

Father removed the stone from Abigail's hand and returned it to the display case on his desk. "I have more to teach you," Father said. "You can do so much more than just that, with time."

Abigail looked at her father but said nothing.

"You won't tell your mother or Evelyn about this," Father said sternly. "This is our secret. Once you are older, you will appreciate these gifts."

***

Abigail's mother, Katherine, knelt in her garden, digging into the soil with a trowel. The Barrett family garden occupied a plot just outside of their home in the countryside, which was itself bordered by a low stone wall. Beyond, a cobbled road ran toward the village. The home was some decades old, but many of the family heirlooms and several pieces of furniture had been passed down to Arthur over several generations.

"Mother, what is in the woods across the river? Father said to never venture there." Abigail stood nearby, watching as her mother planted seeds that would grow into vegetables to set the family's dinner table during the coming summer. Abigail held several seedling packets, which she passed to her mother as the woman gestured for them.

"Oh, no one from the village goes there, that's why. A young girl went missing in those woods a while back. And some people before as well. The constable says it's a treacherous place, with sinkholes and the like."

Katherine stood up and brushed dirt from her apron. She looked down at her younger daughter; Abigail was short and slight, with wavy, light blonde hair and large, expressive brown eyes. She bore no close resemblance to either herself, her husband, or to her older sister Evelyn. "Just be a good girl and do as your father says," Katherine said brusquely. "You don't want to get into any trouble once school lets out."

Abigail followed her mother from the garden into the kitchen, observing Katherine as she removed her gardening gloves and washed her hands with a bar of soap in the kitchen sink. There were several weeks left of school before the summer break, and a classmate, Rachel, had asked Abigail to come with her into the woods to do some exploring.

"You're just scared, admit it! Scared of the woods, like a baby," Rachel had said, sticking her tongue out.

"No, I'm not," Abigail retorted anxiously.

"Well, we can't be friends anymore." Rachel made a face and began to walk away after standing from her spot on the park bench next to Abigail. The village's sole schoolyard was not far away.

"Wait, Rachel, please! I'll go. I want to see the woods too, but my father might find out. He told me to stay away."

Rachel stopped in her tracks, turned around slowly, and then smiled. "No, he won't," she said, her eyes flashing mischievously. "We'll leave for the woods right after our classes. We can hide our bicycles in the bushes near the schoolhouse and then slip away once we're dismissed. Our dads will never find out, nor will anyone else."

The thought of entering those woods, even in the daylight, worried Abigail, but Rachel was one of her few friends. Abigail was at the top of their village's small grammar school, and was ostracized by many of the other pupils because of this. She could have even advanced several years to the upper school, but Abigail's parents had decided against it.

Abigail didn't mind; in fact, she preferred to stay where she was. Certain boys at the upper school had long spread rumors concerning Abigail's father. Arthur Barrett was employed as a journalist and writer, with his articles appearing in various newspapers and publications. Word had reached their village that Mr. Barrett had written for "possibly blasphemous" journals printed overseas, with his articles in either French or German instead of English.

Rachel reassured Abigail: "No one wants to go there, so something must be important about the place. We'll just cross the old bridge, take a look around, and then ride back home on our bikes. We'll have hours of light—it's almost summer, after all!"

Abigail said nothing, but gave a sullen nod.

"Let's get back before they miss us," Rachel chirped, as if distracting Abigail from further discussion. She pulled Abigail up from the bench and took off back toward the village school. Classes would resume after lunch, and final exams were coming up in a few weeks' time.

***

"Hide it here, under the arch." Rachel grimaced as she trudged through the mud and leaned her bicycle against the damp stone of the long bridge that connected the village to the secluded woodlands beyond it. Abigail followed, wheeling her bicycle to the hiding place and propping it near Rachel's. This done, she turned to Rachel, as if awaiting instruction.

Rachel took a sack from her bike's iron basket and opened it to show Abigail the wax paper-wrapped sandwiches inside. "I nabbed these from the school canteen right before we left," she said, handing a sandwich to Abigail. "I'm faster than I look, eh?"

Abigail unwrapped a sandwich and took a bite.

Rachel had already gobbled hers down and was speeding up the river's embankment toward the bridge above. The old stone bridge was not well maintained, but it was solidly built. It had been here for as long as Abigail could remember, and for many years before that.

Unbeknownst to the girls or indeed to any of the villagers, the forest had once been home to a small settlement of shepherds and goat herders. The community had since been abandoned for reasons unknown.

Having caught up with her friend, Abigail peered across to the head of the bridge. It was a warm, cloudy day, the first of summer. Abigail wouldn't be noticed missing until hours from now when Mother would call her for the family dinner.

The forest appeared vast, almost endless, a thick canopy of deciduous trees and rolling hills stretching as far as they could see. Near the end of the bridge was a narrow, partially submerged path leading away into the forest.

"This way," Rachel said, following the path.

Abigail hurried behind her.

The two girls wandered for some time, the bramble undergrowth soon giving way to scores of broad oak trees, their low branches tangled together. The oaks' exposed roots intertwined over the barely visible pathway, slowing the girls' progress. Rachel climbed the raised roots in front of her as she advanced, appearing determined to penetrate to the heart of the woods itself.

After a long while, Abigail stopped. "This is just a deserted place, Rachel. Nothing is here." She wavered briefly and then said, "My mother told me a girl from the village was never found after coming into these woods by herself."

Rachel paused on the path before turning. "She was my cousin, Mary." She showed no emotion as she spoke.

Abigail looked at Rachel in surprise, waiting for her to continue.

"You wouldn't know her—she went to the upper school. It happened when we were quite young. I just wanted to see where it all took place. She'll never be found now."

Abigail's face fell, and she stepped forward to lay a hand on her friend's shoulder. "Rachel, I'm sorry. I only thought you wanted to come here as a dare, for some excitement. I didn't know this was personal for you."

Rachel sat down on the moss-covered roots of a towering oak, a tree that had perhaps seen the previous millennium as a sapling. She looked about the depths of the woods, surveying the maze of trees that stretched in all directions around her.

"You're right," she said after a long moment, her voice strangely quiet, "we should go back. I'm not sure what I wanted to find here, but now I've seen it."

Forcing a smile, Rachel stood and began tracing the path in front of her. Abigail watched her for a moment and made as if to follow, when something caught her eye in the hollow beneath the sprawling oak where Rachel had been seated.

The cavity at the base of the oak contained something. Abigail squinted in the shade, but the hollow was deep and dark, defying the late afternoon sunlight. She approached, crouching beside the roots, and then reached into the oak's dank cavity. It was no good—her arm wasn't long enough. Sighing, Abigail sat back against the oak's roots.

"Rachel, there's something here."

When no response came, Abigail rose, glancing around. She peered down the path Rachel had taken. Nothing.

Pleading under her breath, Abigail took off after her friend. She followed the obscured path for what felt like hours, finally stumbling into a natural formation almost entirely concealed by hanging moss and overgrowth. The formation had an entrance like that of a small cave.

Why didn't we see this the first time through? Abigail thought to herself. *Rachel might be playing a trick on me. Oh, I hope not. There might not even be a Cousin Mary.*

She stepped off the path among the trees and came to the formation's entrance, staring into its dim passageway. The distant sounds of dripping water echoed from somewhere deep inside, and the air within felt cool after the warm summer breeze of the woods. Abigail decided this was a place from which someone might pull a joke on her, so she went in.

The smooth stone passage ended in a woodland grotto, open to the sky above, overgrown, but clearly once used for some purpose. At the center of the grotto was a strange statue. No one else was there.

I hope Rachel didn't fall into one of those crevices Mother warned me about, Abigail thought.

The stone sculpture was very detailed. The figure stood on a pedestal, which was clearly delved from the same quarry as the statue itself. A representation of a bearded, hair-covered man with spiral horns and hooved goat legs, the figure held a set of pipes. Recalling Father's books, Abigail recognized the statue as a Roman faun from classical antiquity.

Has this statue been here since that time? Abigail wondered. *A work of art should be in a museum in London, not out in the woods where no one can see it.*

As she studied the faun's finely wrought face, something moved in the corner of her eye. The wind awoke, the branches of the sturdy elms and green shrubs of the grotto swaying, the clouds above swelling overcast and perilous as they traveled swiftly overhead. The statue extended its arms and placed the set of pipes to its lips. As Abigail staggered back, it began to play a haunting melody.

The song of the pipes drowned out the ominous rumbling of the gathering storm above, its music fixing Abigail in place. Thunder cracked and the winds whipped around her as the eerie yet seductive song swelled to a crescendo. Abigail tore her eyes away, spying something at the grotto's end—an unmoving Rachel spread out on a stone stab, lightning bursting in the sky above her.

Held fast by the pipes' song, Abigail walked to the altar of sacrifice and took in hand the ceremonial blade which rested at the base of the slab. Her wide, staring eyes looked down at the motionless form of Rachel—she was laid on her back, exposed and vulnerable. Tears swelling in her eyes, Abigail felt herself raise the ancient dagger over her head . . .

Evelyn opened her eyes sleepily and looked across at her sister's bed, upon which someone was resting. The curtained window was open, the moonlight shining in from the otherwise lightless country night. Abigail was facing her sister, a blanket draped over her, fast asleep.

Springing from her bed, Evelyn pulled the blanket from Abigail, tossing it to the bedroom floor. Her sister stirred, rolling over from her pillow to look up at Evelyn, still half-asleep.

"Where have you been?" Evelyn hissed angrily. "Mother and Father drove to the village and told the constable you never came home after school. There are men out looking for you at this moment."

Abigail sat up and rubbed her eyes without saying anything, her legs dangling over the side of the bed. In the dim light of the bedroom, Evelyn could see Abigail was still wearing her school dress, which was badly torn and soiled.

"Where am I?" Abigail finally said, her voice barely a whisper.

"You're at home, in our bedroom," replied Evelyn, frowning. "What in God's name happened to you?"

Abigail looked up at Evelyn for the first time and said, "I don't know." Evelyn turned on the nightstand lamp and saw Abigail's shoes lying at the foot of the bed, covered in mud. There was a trail of dirt from the bedroom window to where Abigail had slept.

The sisters heard a door creak open in the house and then hurried footsteps toward the hallway outside of their room. The bedroom door was flung open without warning.

"Abigail!" Katherine exclaimed, running toward the bed and hugging her daughter tightly. "I'm so glad you're safe! We'll let Constable Jarvis know that we've found you." She pushed Abigail away and held her at arm's distance, inspecting her daughter's face and clothes. "But the constable said your friend Rachel is missing as well. Where is she?"

Abigail gazed sluggishly at her mother and then her sister, as if confused by the question. "I can't remember," she said in a dead tone. "I don't even remember how I came home."

Father was now standing in the doorway dressed in his pajamas and slippers, his robe tied at the waist.

"Enough of this. Abigail, go back to sleep once your mother dresses you in your bedclothes." Father shut the bedroom window abruptly, making sure the window latch was locked in place. "I will call on the constable first thing in the morning. The search party can't be reached tonight—not unless I go looking for them myself." With that, he turned and marched from the room.

Katherine began to remove Abigail's dress, and Evelyn took some of her sister's nightclothes out of a drawer. Katherine paused as she lifted the torn dress Abigail was wearing over her daughter's head. She didn't say anything but pulled Abigail's bare arm toward the nightstand's lamp.

There were faint claw marks along her daughter's forearm, as if left by some large animal.

***

"Constable Jarvis discovered your bicycle next to Rachel's under a bridge today. The same bridge to the woods your father and I warned you not to enter." Katherine was somber as she relayed the news to Abigail. "This means you could be implicated in a crime if Rachel isn't found, even as a young girl."

Abigail positioned herself on a stool in the kitchen, listening to her mother intently. Abigail looked out the kitchen window and saw Evelyn working in the family garden. *Where is Father?* she thought.

She met her mother's eyes. "How, Mother? Rachel and I are friends—I loved her dearly."

"The constable's men will continue to search for Rachel, but it was explained to me there is the possibility of a criminal case if any more evidence against you is found. I will pray for both of us."

Katherine studied Abigail. She knew her young daughter couldn't have anything to do with Rachel's disappearance. Yes, her selective amnesia was disconcerting, but her condition, real or feigned, didn't mean she had actually harmed her friend.

"You can't recall how your bike ended up under the bridge? You were riding home from school, you stopped by the side of the road with Rachel, and then the next thing you remember is waking up in your bedroom at night?"

"Yes, Mother, that's all I remember. Now may I please go outside with Evelyn?" Abigail dropped from the stool and stood near the kitchen table, waiting to be dismissed.

"Go. But dinner will be ready in a few hours—once your father returns. The constable will want to speak with you again in a couple of days when the search is concluded." Katherine watched her daughter open the kitchen's side door and join her sister in the garden. There were already insinuations being made in the village about this apparent tragedy, with some of the villagers singling out Abigail as the culprit.

"You're a witch!" One of the boys threw a stone at Abigail, but it missed her, striking the tree behind instead. "And you killed Rachel!" Several older boys with handfuls of stones had cornered Abigail outside the schoolyard against a shady tree. Abigail moved to walk past them, but they blocked her exit.

"I'm telling Mrs. Thorpe!" Abigail cried out. She became very frightened as the three boys glared down at her and, despite herself, she began to cry. One of the boys turned and swore under his breath. Mrs. Thorpe was walking toward them at a brisk pace, her face as fearsome as ever. "It's that old bag, Mrs. Thorpe. Just walk away, don't look at her," he commanded.

Quickly, the boys slipped behind the tree where Abigail was cornered and then away from the school grounds.

"Abigail, are you all right?" Mrs. Thorpe crouched down beside her. "Do you know those boys' names? What class are they in?"

"No, but . . ." Abigail hesitated. This wasn't the first such incident. Most of the children at school had coolly ignored Abigail after Rachel disappeared, their parents telling them Abigail may have been to blame after word circulated through the village. Now, with yet another reason to resent her, their coldness was apparently turning to outright hostility. The last thing Abigail wanted was more trouble.

"No," she corrected herself, "I don't know who they are. They're in another class, but I'm not sure which one. I didn't get a good look at them as it happened so fast."

Mrs. Thorpe frowned, but decided not to push the matter. She moved to calm Abigail and said, "Just come back to the yard. You need to collect your things before heading home. You must let me know if something like this happens again."

Abigail watched as Mrs. Thorpe walked back to gather the other children in the schoolyard and lead them back inside. She reached down and picked up the stone that had nearly struck her from the foot of the tree. Red-faced from crying, Abigail squeezed tightly, then released her hand. The small grey toad croaked, and Abigail placed it into her dress pocket before walking back to the village school.

***

Abigail pressed her ear against her parent's bedroom door. The hallway was dark—she was supposed to be asleep. Mother and Father had been arguing, so she'd crept down the hall to find out if they were discussing anything that might involve her. Evelyn was still deep in slumber, oblivious to her parents' raised voices.

"I've never felt right about Abigail. You know that, Arthur. Even my pregnancy with her was quite . . . difficult."

There was a pause.

"There were terrible nightmares up until her birth. You must remember how it was. I vowed I would never have another child after Abigail."

"Yes, but the doctor said nothing was wrong with you, at least not physically," Arthur replied. "He said it was all depression from a second pregnancy so soon after your first."

Abigail peered through the keyhole and caught a glimpse of her father trying to pull her mother close, only for her to move to the other side of their bed, glancing away from him.

"But here is the good news I promised you," her father continued, undeterred, "I've accepted an editorial position with *The Daily Sentinel*, the paper I told you about when we first considered moving away from Wiltshire. Relocating overseas will require applying for family passports, visas, and eventually new citizenship once we're settled in."

Katherine turned to face him again, and he smiled at her hopefully. "Arthur, I couldn't be more happy," she said, smiling weakly. "We need a fresh start after all of this. Even our friends no longer see us. We're not welcome here anymore."

She embraced her husband, and they sat down on the bed, Katherine resting her head on Arthur's shoulder.

"This is a permanent move; we'll be far away from Wiltshire," Arthur said, caressing Katherine's hair. "A new life in a new country. I'll be in the study for a while to go over some of the details. Try to get some sleep; I'll join you soon."

Abigail backed away as if struck and quickly dodged down the hallway, silently slipping into her bedroom and leaping into bed. A moment later, Arthur's head appeared in the bedroom doorway. He glanced at each bed in turn and, apparently satisfied, continued on toward his study.

He sat at his writing desk and reviewed the family's travel documents, considering how taking Abigail away from Wiltshire had changed the plans he had for her. Abigail would still one day reach her full potential under his tutelage as an Ovate. Too many of the villagers and local authorities had begun to suspect the truth—or at least part of it, including Katherine.

Arthur stood and selected a black leather-bound volume from among the many books lining the shelves of his study. The weighty tome was centuries old, with a golden sickle on its spine.

Returning to his desk, Arthur began to quietly read aloud, murmuring in a strange language. The wind outside the study's bay window stirred, the sudden rush of night air rattling the aged glass of its windowpanes.

Katherine lay on her bed half-asleep, breathing lightly. She reflected on the move from Wiltshire. Life in a new country, her husband with a new position, and a fresh start away from the enmity and social isolation that had plagued their family these last months.

Abigail must have gone into those woods, she thought, but could she really be the cause of Rachel's disappearance? Shortly before she realized she was pregnant with Abigail, and then throughout the term of her pregnancy, Katherine had suffered from a recurrent nightmare: a grove in the woods at twilight, a stone stab, and shadowy forms surrounding her.

Each time, the nightmare would play out in the same manner. Barefoot and in a sheer white gown, she would lie on the stone slab. A man (or was it a man?) appeared from among the dark forms and stood before her. She would awaken just as the man had knelt over her, reaching out with a clawed hand . . .

The first time the nightmare came upon her, she'd awoken the next morning with odd scratches on her arms and legs, but the marks had quickly faded. Afterward, she'd begun to feel a visceral craving for raw meat and organs from the butcher's, the purchases of which she hid from Arthur. Sharp pains, as if she were being kicked by some hooved animal inside her, persisted through the pregnancy, even though the doctor could find nothing wrong.

Katherine lay on her back, touching her stomach as she recalled her fear the unborn child would suffer a deformity or even be monstrous once delivered. But Abigail had been perfectly healthy as a baby—beautiful, even.

Yet there was always the lingering suspicion that something was wrong with Abigail. The moments when Katherine would catch her daughter studying her while they worked together in the garden or in the kitchen, a puzzling expression on her face. Abigail's frequent nighttime walks alone these last few years, and the sometimes-fitful sleeps she endured, waking Katherine in the middle of the night to find her daughter wide-eyed and terrified. Could Abigail, this lovely young girl, truly be a murderess?

Abigail was asleep, tucked up warmly in her bed. Outside her bedroom window, amid the moaning winds, the cloaked figure of a tall man stood in silence. The outline of stag's antlers protruded sharply from the tall man's head as he stared in through the window at Abigail. Abigail continued to sleep, oblivious to the man's presence.

***

Abigail peered around at Father's new study, which had been left open and unlocked. She held an oakwood cane across her lap, the length of which she examined, running her hand over its burnished shaft. The cane wore a silver metal handle in the shape of a ram's head with horns. She could hear her mother, who'd just been on the telephone, sobbing in the nearby living room.

The crying stopped. A moment later, Katherine walked into the study. Abigail quickly hid her father's cane under the writing desk.

"We will likely have to move to a rented home soon, Abigail," Katherine said, her eyes almost bloodshot. "I won't be able to keep up with the mortgage now that your father is gone. I'm sorry. I wanted better for you and your sister."

She let herself fall in front of Abigail's chair and hugged her child close, tears leaking down her cheeks. Finally, she straightened, sniffed, and dabbed at her eyes. "It's getting late. Go upstairs and get some rest. Evelyn is already asleep. The doctor gave me enough sedatives for her to last the next month."

Abigail slipped from the plush chair and stood in front of her mother, giving her a faint smile, as if to assent. Her mother slipped past her, and Abigail heard the bathroom door down the hallway shut, followed by sounds of incessant crying.

Out the study's window, the spacious yard stretched behind the house, obscured from their neighbors by rows of oak trees on either side. Mother had found Father hanging from a branch by a knotted rope among the copse of oaks at the yard's far end. The police had removed Father's body from the tree before Abigail and Evelyn had arrived home from school.

The night before, Father had called Abigail to his study in the family's new home, coming first to her room where she'd been reading alone. Father had seemed very distraught, his eyes wide with fear, his face pallid and grieved.

She'd followed him to his study, noting the heavy curtains of its picture window were drawn, blocking the panoramic view of the back garden. A jumbled pile of books lay on Father's desk, a black book with a gold sickle on its spine being the most prominent. It was as if the books had been torn from the study's shelves in a panic and then searched through, one after the other.

Arthur took Abigail by both arms. "Abigail, I'm not sure how to tell you this, but I must. You have a very special gift. Not one received from me, but from your real father." His breath came in ragged gasps, but he composed himself enough to continue: "There are sacraments of evil as well as of good in all of us, but how we choose to use these graces determines our fates. There are also places where shadows and the dwellers of twilight reach out to touch this world, if only imperceptibly. I started you on a path that may lead to a world of shadows, but—for your own sake—choose a different one once I am gone."

Holding a trembling hand to Abigail's cheek, Arthur kissed her goodnight. Finally, he led her to the study's door and then locked himself inside. Abigail returned to her bedroom to sleep.

Now, she rose from the writing desk and unlatched the study's back door. She walked to the sheltered copse where Arthur had hanged himself by the neck. There, among the oak trees, stood the Horned God. He embraced Abigail, and she embraced him in return.

Cirque des Plus Grands Mystères

There was no light in the coffin, and not much more air. Clarence writhed in the tight, confined space as he surfaced suddenly into horrible consciousness. At once, he pulled his leaden arms from his sides and onto his chest and began pressing against the lid of the coffin with the palms of his hands, becoming more frantic with each faltering push. His own jagged, raspy breath was the only sound Clarence could hear over the cracking of his fingernails as they broke into the overhead enclosure of his buried prison.

Splinters of pine fell onto his parched mouth and forehead, threatening to slip into his eyes. Searing pain bit into him as his fingertips shredded against the wood, with thin streams of blood running over his hands and onto his face. Despite the total blackness of the coffin, Clarence sensed his vision was clouding with each halting, panicked breath. How much time did he have left?

There were muffled noises above him. The garbled intonation of men speaking and then a commotion of vigorous, hurried digging. Clarence paused and lay still, trying to preserve his last remaining breaths. As he drifted into unconsciousness, a shovelhead broke through the wood coffin lid, and a flood of humid, tropical air rushed over him . . .

The window of his fourth-floor hotel room was unlatched and open, offering Clarence a late-night view of the city and its port.

At once, he sprang up in bed, crying out. Nothing—there was nothing. It had just been a dream. He exhaled, perched on the edge of the mattress, and sucked in a deep, deliberate breath. The sheets were damp with sweat, the night's moist air hanging over him.

The nightmare had returned, and so soon after the last one. Each time, Clarence dreamed of being buried alive and then dug up by some unknown interlopers. Yet it was the immediacy of this most recent burial ordeal that surprised him; his passenger ship had docked on the island only this past morning, and this frightful vision of vivisepulture had invaded his dreams the very same night.

The recurring nightmare had been with Clarence since he'd first landed on this ill-fated island several years prior, but tonight's episode had been the most vivid yet. He always got a sense that the burial was occurring somewhere on the island itself, but so little could be grasped from the dream—there was just a dark coffin, his terror at being buried alive, and the men breaking in with a shovel just before he awoke.

Clarence poured tepid water from the pitcher on the worn table across from his bed. He refilled the pitcher and washed his stubbled face before drying himself with a rough cloth. The ceramic toilet set and the ornately carved table had seen better days, but still retained some of their original colonial elegance. Few visitors came to this island, but those who did most often sought their fortunes—even at the risk of their lives.

***

The early morning bustle on the street outside the hotel stirred Clarence from the shallow, fitful sleep he'd found after waking from the nightmare. He was to meet a man at *Café la Plantation* to discuss the shipping of contraband goods off the island. The coastal city on the other side of the calm, green-blue sea was the goods' destination.

The island was a haven for sellers of illicit cargo, possessing little in the way of effective government and even less in the way of law enforcement. The last of the occupying foreign soldiers were leaving the island for good and, in their absence, a void of any unifying authority.

Clarence stood in front of the oval floor mirror resting on an upright frame near the room's door. He'd not bothered shaving, and had dressed in a white summer suit and straw boater hat. He adjusted a silk necktie under his pressed shirt collar.

The faint dark circles under his eyes betrayed Clarence's sleeplessness, but he hoped Junior wouldn't notice. He and Junior had done business on several occasions, and it was Clarence's heartfelt wish this would be the last time he would make the journey to the island.

The handful of runs Junior had conducted with Clarence had always been from the eastern part of the island, which was a separate, autonomous nation unto itself. If the pending deal with Junior was closed, it would set Clarence up in relative comfort, and he could abandon the smuggling life for some less risky line of work.

The mirror's glass was very polished, in sharp contrast to the otherwise dingy hotel room. This cheval mirror might have even been lifted at some point from one of the many ruined plantations in the island's interior.

Giving himself one final glance over, Clarence reached out to touch the glass. His reflection distorted as the mirror began to tilt upward. He looked down as it pivoted toward him and saw his reflection, now a mass of liquescent flesh, tumorous and suppurating, crawling with turgid maggots.

Clarence grasped the border of the mirror and held it tightly, staring into the silvery glass. The horror was gone; his face's reflection was finely wrinkled and weathered but hale, as it had been only a moment before.

A chill came over Clarence as he thought on the repulsive visage. "Nerves, that's all it was," Clarence assured himself, "bad dreams are chasing me even into daytime. A shot of vermouth at *Café la Plantation* will do me good."

The street outside the hotel was filled with vendors, men pushing produce carts, and women carrying baskets on their heads. The scent of ripe fruit mixed with the foul air of the city washed over Clarence as he stepped out, the fetid aroma accentuated by the humid climate. *Café la Plantation* was but a few city blocks over from the hotel.

"In dollars, not francs, like you asked." Clarence placed the dull brown paper envelope on the café table and grabbed a peeling wooden chair from nearby, seating himself across from Junior.

"And good day to you as well, Clarence. Where are your manners?" Junior said in heavily accented English. He smiled broadly, quickly reaching across the table and stuffing the envelope into his pants pocket, glancing around the café as he did so.

Clarence replied, "*Bonjour*, *Monsieur* Junior. You look well. The molasses trade must have been good to you of late, especially now prohibition is done."

Junior wrinkled his forehead and leaned into the table. "*Monsieur* Clarence, I have to say, I'm surprised to see you back. Maybe the money was just too good to pass up, no?"

Clarence recalled his first meeting with Junior and the dangerous runs they had completed together: moving alcohol and sugarcane molasses to the mainland at great risk to their safety and the lives of their crew. Junior had guts, but Clarence had never fully learned to trust him, and now was no exception.

Junior had been born and raised on the island but had learned English from "your army men and a missionary schoolteacher." He was a young man, vigorous and self-assured, but always cloaked in uncertainty; Junior was a wild card even among the tumultuous environs of the island. Clarence still did not even know Junior's given name, as he had never revealed it.

Clarence looked directly at Junior. "Like you, I'm getting squeezed by the new laws on booze. Why would someone buy from us when it's now legal and on the shelves again? But we can still undercut the competition on molasses; no tariffs, no taxes, so lower prices for our customers. This is a buy I can't pass up."

A waiter came to their table and Clarence ordered a shot of vermouth.

Junior waited for the waiter to leave before leaning back in his seat and grinning. "We'll meet tonight at the docks not far from here and take an old tug up the coast. The loading place is in a jungle spot I've used before, where no one will look for us. The streets will be empty—this is the first night of the Feast of Souls. Everyone will be inside their homes or at the cemeteries, so you don't have to worry about being followed.

"The whole cargo will be placed on your sea-worthy ship and, from there, you can take it back home. Your crew will be on that ship, *Monsieur* Clarence?"

Clarence nodded, trying to keep his face unreadable. "They were paid in part before I left and will be there. Just a skeleton crew—after all, we want to involve as few as possible. I'm much more careful now than I was in the past. Your people will supply the labor to load the goods, I take it?"

Junior's face twitched, but before he could speak, the waiter returned. He took a crystal shot glass from his tray and placed it in front of Clarence before turning and departing.

"Yes, *Monsieur* Clarence," Junior said, his composure restored, "you don't worry about that. Our men will never breathe a word, I promise you. See you at nine o'clock."

Clarence walked back to his hotel, feeling a bit lighter now that the first part of his last trip was done. The taste of the vermouth lingered in his mouth, and now he needed some breakfast. The hotel had a small dining room where he could get a plate of eggs with plantains. The late morning and afternoon would provide the time for Clarence to read the sale papers he had brought with him and plot out what would happen to this sizable shipment once he was back in port.

The morning and afternoon passed quickly. Clarence spent the time working at the table in his room and had lunch brought up to him from the hotel kitchen. Papers were spread over the makeshift desk, with his open leather journal displaying the figures he had calculated and jotted down. Junior had received the advance payment, and the rest would be paid to the smuggling crew's captain once Clarence took possession of his cargo.

He finished what was left of his lunch for supper and then prepared to go down to the docks to meet Junior. The late autumn sun was beginning to set over the horizon and rosy-fleeced light spilled in through the open window of his hotel room. Clarence sat on his bed and looked out over the city and to the sea beyond it, knowing it would soon be dark. The streets would be deserted, just as Junior had said—tonight was the first night of the festival.

"Will you be back soon, *Mesye*?" The woman at the hotel's front desk said as Clarence walked by her station. "Tonight's not a good night to be out on those streets, especially for a Yankee. Why don't you just get some sleep instead?"

Clarence could see the young woman was genuinely concerned, so he stopped and shot her a reassuring smile. "A friend told me there's a festival tonight, a feast for the dead. I'd heard about it during other visits, but I was never here when the festival took place. People were always reluctant to speak of what went on. I'm eager to see what all the fuss is about."

From here, the streets outside appeared pitch black, with no signs of lights from other buildings or passersby. The weather had cooled, a balmy breeze wafting through the hotel's yellow-painted double doors and over Clarence and the young woman. She leaned forward from the check-in counter, her long, curly, reddish hair loose, spilling down her heavily freckled face. Her expression was now quite anxious.

"You are right, *Mesye*. It is the *Fet Gede*, the night when the world of the dead and the world of the living are closest. During the day, the people were in the streets, but now they are seeing their families who have passed on. But who knows who is out there? I tell you, it's not safe."

"Restless spirits?" Clarence was just about able to hide his amusement. "I'm just meeting someone. I'll stick to the main thoroughfare as a precaution. But thanks for your concern; I appreciate it."

Despairing, the woman breathed in a hoarse whisper, "It's the *Culte des Mortes*, *Mesye*. *Jaden Dyab la a*. The Devil's Garden. Stay away from the graveyards this night and the next, no matter who invites you there. I will pray that *les Saints Bénis* keep you."

Clarence gave her a final confused smile before turning and sauntering out onto the empty street of the hotel district. The woman watched him go, her sad eyes boring into his back until, at last, the darkness swallowed him.

***

The hard-packed dirt streets of the city were ill-maintained, but an extensive tram system ran through the downtown area and its adjacent districts, which belied the abject poverty of the capital and of the island itself. The public trams had ceased running several hours ago, and Clarence proceeded on foot to his appointment with Junior.

Single lights, probably candles, flickered in the open windows of tenement homes, but otherwise, the streets were sheltered in darkness. The moon was only a waning crescent but provided most of the remaining illumination from its perch in the cloudy night sky. In the distance, Clarence spied a long procession of lights advancing in single-file out of the city, but he was too far away to make out any more than that.

Turning a street corner, Clarence was nearing his destination. The waterfront had recently undergone new construction, and a concrete wharf had been added, which extended ahead of the antiquated wooden docks built during the city's founding. As he paused in front of a dilapidated shipwright's warehouse near the open avenue, a shadow cast itself over him, seemingly from nowhere.

Clarence looked around and saw nothing. The street was quiet and empty. He took out a packet of *Gaulois Bleu* from his coat's front pocket and lit one with his silver lighter, taking a long drag before continuing on. Only moments later, he paused again, a shadow casting itself into his path, this time from behind. It was larger now, and it had a shape: the shape of a man.

Clarence turned and again saw nothing. Did someone know about his meeting with Junior? Perhaps a rival smuggler? Clarence never carried a weapon—he had always feared arrest more than robbers—but now, and not for the first time, he regretted being without a gun.

Spinning back around, he hurried on, pulling his jacket tight around him despite the warm evening. The nighttime sea stretched out to his right, its cresting waves glimmering in the faint moonlight, and he traced a route along the edge of the water by the docks. The docks were destitute, the cluster of ships parked in the city's harbor without occupants. If someone was planning on attempting to waylay him, he would have to make a run for the hotel, which was now blocks away.

There was someone in the distance. A figure stood near a tugboat moored to the dock, their features not yet visible in the dim light. The boat bobbed slightly in the warm sea wind, and Clarence hurried his step. An enormous shadow spread itself across his path as he moved, the outline of the figure's top hat and long-sleeved coat now clear. Clarence froze and stared at the animated silhouette which abruptly gestured to him, tipping its hat and then waving a hand in a gesture of farewell.

The shadow receded behind a stack of shipping crates and barrels, slowly retreating from Clarence's view. When he looked up, he found Junior walking toward him.

"*Monsieur* Clarence, what is that expression on your face? You see your dead papa or something?" Junior's smirk was obvious even in the low light.

"I . . . I just saw a man. I think he was following me." Clarence felt uneasy, steadying himself as he tossed his spent cigarette butt into the gently churning waves splashing up against the mooring poles.

"There is no man, Clarence. No one is here. Just us and the souls of the dead who roam this night. Let's get on the boat; the crew is waiting."

Clarence quickly scanned the docks before following Junior down the boarding ramp and onto the tugboat. The boat's captain was behind the tug's helm, but none of the other crewmen showed themselves.

Junior unmoored the tug from the docks, throwing the length of rope back onto the ramp as the captain nodded and started the boat's engine. The engine sputtered and convulsed for a moment before chugging along at an even pace. At last, the tug drifted away from the docks and out to sea, gaining speed as the harbor grew smaller. Once they were past the city's limits, they made a hard turn toward the shore.

The tugboat parted the murky waters, white-capped frothing waves breaking from its port and starboard sides. The tug's destination was a remote and mostly uncharted jungle clearing near the island's sparsely populated interior.

The night sky had become clear, and Clarence stood at the tugboat's bow, gazing up into the starry canopy above him, nearly lost in thought. He heard Junior say something to the captain from the bridge behind him, but the chugging of the tug's engine drowned out the words.

"There are no excuses! You men are just lazy rats."

The four crew members stared up at Clarence sullenly as he berated them.

"We're behind schedule now, because of this." Clarence stood in front of the men as the sun began to set over the sea behind him, looking down at them from the chartered merchant ship's main hatch. Clarence had hired the ship and its crew to transport this run of illicit goods from the island, but the ship's captain wasn't entirely clear on the nature of the cargo.

Normally a very silent man, the ship's first mate spoke up. "We only did as you asked us. You were wrong about how long loading the ship would take. There was more cargo than what was written on the shipper's ledger." The first mate was an experienced seaman—taciturn, rough, and haggard—but was articulate in his own way.

Clarence sighed, his anger dissipating. "I went by what the suppliers' estimate. Now let's get this finished and be on our way. I'm losing money as we bicker over this mess." Clarence stepped down and walked away, ignoring the glare the first mate gave him as he descended the ship's stairs to his quarters below deck.

This was not the first time Clarence had spoken harshly to the crew; he and the captain had maintained a working relationship that had lasted several years. Clarence had cultivated a reputation for callousness, even cruelty, among the captain's sailors, and the men had quickly grown to resent him. This commercial ship had run most of his biggest jobs from the island during prohibition.

The chartered ship would leave port that evening on a voyage due to last almost a week. The trip would end with a late-night docking in the waters outside the discharge port. The cargo would then be transported to shore on smaller, more nimble vessels so the goods could evade customs. Clarence wasn't sure if the ship's crew knew the value of the cargo they were carrying, but the ship's captain was a long-time retainer, and Clarence believed he could be trusted.

There was a knock at the cabin door. "Clarence, may I have a word with you?" It was the gruff voice of the ship's captain.

"Please, come in," Clarence replied without rising from his desk.

The door opened and the captain entered, his bearded face shadowy in the low light of the Bakelite desk lamp. "The men are becoming angry and frustrated," the captain announced. "First Mate Dorman came to me and said they are being overworked. That you are pushing them too hard to make an impossible schedule." The captain was an older man who'd spent many years at sea, and often left Clarence to supervise the crew while they loaded and unloaded his goods.

"Not true at all, Captain Hancock," was Clarence's measured response. "It's the men's fault we're behind as they didn't follow the schedule. If we're late to the offshore meet-up point, the handlers won't be there with the boats. No boats, no way to get the cargo to shore. We'd have to turn around and go back out to sea."

Captain Hancock stepped back and seemed to be weighing something up in his head. Clarence knew he was a valuable client and that the captain knew a serious disagreement with him might very well lead to his business being taken elsewhere. "I'll see what I can do with the men. You're right—we can't miss the drop-off point or it will cost us all."

The captain tipped his peaked cap to Clarence and then slowly closed the cabin door. The muffled sound of the captain's footsteps echoed from the stairwell and then, for a few moments, from the deck above. Clarence sat and stared at the closed door as the footsteps faded, returning to the task at hand only once they were gone.

With his bookkeeping ledgers open in front of him, Clarence noted with satisfaction that this shipment of rum, molasses, and spices would be his most lucrative yet. The final sale of these goods would elevate Clarence's smuggling business into a new class of operation. He would no longer need to retain Captain Hancock with his aging watercraft and surly crew; he would be able to afford a ship of his own and his own men. Clarence wondered with some amusement whether Captain Hancock's crew were tempted to mutiny, given how large a sum of money was involved in this transaction. Did Hancock's men understand the full worth of what was being shipped?

The sound of footsteps and a hurried knock abruptly broke Clarence's stream of thought. A voice spoke from the other side of the cabin door: "We are docking to refuel, Mr. Morris. Please come above deck in fifteen minutes."

Clarence stood and rushed to open the door. A young man—a member of the crew—stood in front of him.

"Fifteen minutes, sir. We need to stop before going out to sea."

Clarence gripped the edge of the open door in frustration. He sputtered angrily, "There was no scheduled stop. Who approved this?"

The crewman replied, "First Mate Dorman, sir. We didn't have time to refuel due to all hands on the loading dock, so we are stopping now."

Slamming the door without a word, Clarence returned to his desk. He gathered his business papers and put them into the desk's top drawer, locking the drawer with the small key he kept on a chain around his neck. Clarence glanced at his reflection in the cabin's framed wall mirror and placed his straw boater hat on his head. As he turned his back on the mirror to leave, a caliginous shape, darkling and nebulous, began to form within the mirror's surface.

The ship had made slow progress along the island's coast and was now far from a port of any size. Clarence stood on the upper deck and gazed out at the sea, its waves sparkling in the bright moonlight of the evening. Their modestly sized steamship was headed toward a set of wooden piers, exhaust smoke trailing from its twin funnels. The piers protruded into the shallow waters of the jungle's shoreline; standing atop them were several men who appeared to be waiting for them.

The ship docked, and the men began moving barrels from the adjacent pier to the ship: fuel for the oil-fired steam boilers. Clarence saw that Captain Hancock and First Mate Dorman were already on the shore, moving between tents pitched in the clearing and speaking with some of the local men. Clarence walked up the two makeshift planks connecting the ship to the pier and sought out the clump of tents nestled at the fore of the jungle's tangled undergrowth.

"Come sit with us, Clarence. Armand here is going to share some of his spiced rum." Captain Hancock was in a jovial mood; he seemed a different man to the old captain who'd questioned Clarence earlier. Clarence seated himself on one of the folding canvas chairs in front of the camp's main tent, between the captain and first mate.

The captain placed a coarse hand on Clarence's shoulder, reassuring him. "Our ship should be ready within the hour, and you can get some rest after a nightcap. Here, drink up." The young man Captain Hancock had introduced as Armand handed Clarence a drink in a glass tumbler.

"Thanks," offered Clarence as he took his first shallow sip from the green enameled tumbler. Strong stuff—the spice was almost cloying to Clarence's palate.

Clarence studied the campsite beyond the open fire, the only source of light nearby besides the oil lamps that hung from posts dotting the camp. Some of the laborers were standing nearby, restless and shifty. Clarence took another drink from the tumbler, noting Captain Hancock was holding an empty glass.

"Mr. Morris, you seem sleepy. Why don't you finish your rum and then head to the ship? We'll be embarking soon." First Mate Dorman hovered near Clarence's chair. His voice was acerbic, almost mocking in tone, his timeworn features hollow in the light of the flickering flames.

Clarence put the tumbler to his lips, but it fell from his hand, the remaining rum spilling out over his clothes. He tried to stand but felt dizzy, dropping back onto the flimsy chair behind him. Slowly, he slid onto the sandy ground.

He felt hands take hold of his deadened limbs, lifting him up . . .

But what happened next? Clarence looked away from the tugboat's bow and up into the late-night sky again, as if waking from a trance. Junior called to him: "*Monsieur* Clarence, the captain wishes to have a word with you."

The times that followed that night at the camp had not been good ones. Clarence never recovered his cargo, which set him back years financially. His succeeding memory was of wandering along a deserted beach in the early morning, his mouth and skin parched, his white suit soiled and torn.

Clarence had found his way from the beach to a small town several miles away and hitched a ride on a cart back to the city. Days had passed unaccounted for. Accepting a loan from a business associate, Clarence purchased a ticket on a steamer headed home. He never saw Captain Hancock or his crew again.

***

The isolated cove consisted of a natural clearing in the jungle, a white sandy beach, and a single but sturdy pier lit by hanging lanterns extending out into the littoral waters. The tugboat docked, and Junior roped it securely to its moorings. Clarence stepped from the creaky deck onto the pier from a raised plank and peered around. The sandy beach was empty, but a trail led off into the jungle from which flickering lights were visible.

Clarence hadn't seen anyone else on the tug besides Junior and the tug's captain. Also, where were his hired ship and its crew?

Turning, Clarence saw Junior disappearing down the trail and into the jungle. The outline of his moving form was barely visible against the shelter of the tree ferns and tall hardwoods lining the pathway. Clarence stepped onto the stretch of fine sand in front of him, crossing the threshold from the shore to the jungle clearing, and then stepped onto the trail, following Junior.

The tropical forest around him was very active, humming with the ambient nighttime sounds of insect life. Clarence stopped to remove his boater hat and wipe the accumulated sweat from this brow. Where was Junior? He could no longer see him up ahead.

He emerged onto another clearing surrounded by jungle, lit only by a small bonfire at its center. As Clarence approached, erratic shadows danced in the grass, and large, exaggerated shapes loomed amid the trees.

Clarence saw a line of ragged men lifting crates and barrels onto a series of rolling flatbed carts, the carts having been perhaps retrieved from some derelict railway station. The men's actions were stiff and awkward, their steps mechanical and halting. As Clarence drew closer, he could see all of them were very gaunt, with sunken eyes and ashen complexions.

There was a rustling noise from among the ferns close to the trail. From behind Clarence, another of the gaunt men trod out of the jungle, his pallid face impassive and unblinking. Without noticing Clarence, he shambled past him across the clearing and took up the trail's path, which continued at the clearing's far side. The macabre figure was carrying something—it laid across his outstretched arms.

Clarence watched the gaunt man for a brief time before following at a distance behind him. Maybe, he reasoned, the man would lead him to Junior.

The trail snaked through the dense jungle, leading up a shallow hill and then back down again to the jungle floor. Upon descending, Clarence saw the crumbling edifice of a once-stately plantation, its former palatial splendor evident even now.

The gaunt man made his way up the vine-strewn steps of the plantation's columnated exterior and then through its partially open doors, vanishing from view. Clarence paused at the base of the hill and examined the grand building. The broken windows of both floors showed no light within; only the muted illumination of the crescent moon through the jungle canopy revealed any details of the abandoned dwelling.

Clarence hurried across the half-buried cobblestone path to the wide double doors. He pushed inside and paused at the foot of a blighted imperial staircase. Clarence could see the plantation house had indeed been a grand château for its master—gilded portraits hung on every wall, and a ballroom adjacent to the foyer stretched off into shadow. Clarence listened for the sound of footsteps, but none could be heard.

He eased past the cracked rococo doors of the ballroom. In its center stood a strange thing: a large cheval mirror, very similar to the one in his hotel room but much heavier and of more elaborate design. Resting about the mirror were many fetishes and unlit votive candles, black and sickly in color. The mirror was both repulsive and attractive at once, and Clarence was drawn toward it.

"There you are, *Monsieur* Clarence. We've been waiting for you."

Clarence turned sharply to see Junior stepping out of the shadows of the ballroom's interior. His face was painted chalky white, with thick black lines framing his eyes and mouth.

The votive candles surrounding the mirror flared and began burning brightly, revealing the other men who had formed a wide ring around Clarence. The men's faces were painted in the same ritual fashion as Junior's, the make-up resembling a kind of death mask. They stood silently, as if waiting for someone's arrival.

Distant drums began to beat somewhere outside, their rhythms swelling and rising. Clarence eyed the men assembled before him, licking his lips and trying to count them—fifteen maybe, or more. At once, he bolted, barreling past Junior, but two men—God, they were fast—seized him by the arms and dragged him back. They threw him down before the mirror, in which a shape as black as a funeral pall was now forming.

Looking away, Clarence shut his eyes and clasped his ears to shield them from the manic cadence of the rising drums. The sound grew louder, filling the space of the gutted ballroom. Clarence gasped, sweat beading on his skin, his head jerking in a panicked spasm toward the mirror as an enormous shadow cast itself between him and this portal to the world of the dead.

Junior spoke in a clear, powerful voice: "Papa called you back from across the sea, Clarence. That is why you were having those dreams. Your men betrayed you, gave you to Papa to make into one of his servants. You came to your senses once you were pulled out of the ground, and you got away. No one's ever done that before, I'll give you that.

"But now you are here, and Papa will collect what is his on this night, the night when the world of the dead and the world of the living are closest."

Clarence panted and gulped, his terror tightening in his throat. Then, finding the strength to speak, he shouted above the din of the drums, "What is his? What of mine is Papa's?"

Junior smirked and then nodded toward the mirror. "Why, your soul, *Monsieur* Clarence. Papa wants your soul."

A pair of massive arms reached out of the mirror, stygian as the night, and seized Clarence around the waist.

Clarence let out a scream, its sound nearly drowned out by the wildly thrashing drums, his body pulled into the mercury surface of the mirror. He seemed to melt away piece by piece, until only a single straining hand remained, clawing at nothing. Soon, that too disappeared into the netherworld of the mirror.

Far-off cries echoed from somewhere, and at once, the beating drums fell silent. Junior stepped toward the now-dormant mirror, touching his fingers to the glass.

***

The gaunt men labored near the spent bonfire, having worked throughout the night. Their task was almost done, and rays of morning sunlight were scattered through the giant fronds of the tree ferns sheltering the jungle clearing. The cargo was assembled, loaded onto the flatbed carts; it was almost ready to be pushed across the long trail of wooden planks set back to the beach. A newly arrived commercial steamer was docked at the pier.

Junior stood at the planks' end, where the sandy beach met the pier. He lit a *Gauloises* taken from a packet in his pocket and adjusted the straw boater hat on his head. The steamer's captain walked up the ramp from his ship and raised an arm in greeting.

"Good morning," the captain called out. "What a night it was! We were well ahead of schedule when a terrible storm came out of nowhere." The captain was young but was not a novice seaman. He and his crew had been badly shaken by a ferocious tempest which had beset them the previous night, the likes of which they had never seen before.

Junior flashed a grin. "Strange—we waited for you, but you never came. The sea was peaceful at these shores, like the way I sleep at night." He ambled his way across the planks to join the captain on the pier.

The captain eyed Junior as he approached, frowning slightly. "Even our radio signal was jammed. The waters to these ports are usually so calm, like you said, but we were tossed on the waves for hours. I was sure we were done for when the storm just rolled back, almost as quickly as it had come, exactly at midnight." Removing his seaman's cap for a moment, the captain wiped his brow with a cloth he kept in his trouser pocket, the heat from the island's morning sun already bearing down on him.

Junior held his lit cigarette between two fingers and offered the captain one, which the man accepted. "Mr. Morris had to leave very early this morning," Junior said. "Business matters that couldn't wait another day. We'll load the steamer's hold with his cargo, and you can be on your way."

The captain nodded, took a shaky puff from the *Gauloises*, and, without a word, turned to walk back down the ramp to the deck of his ship. Junior strolled along the planks to the hidden clearing in the jungle and found his older brother, Armand, at work. Armand was herding the ghastly troupe of laborers back into the plantation house where the steamer's crew wouldn't see them. He and Junior would then push the full carts to the pier and help the crew unload the cargo.

"Hey, Bénison, where you get the *blanc* from?" Armand gestured toward one of the gaunt men shuffling near the end of the line. The man had the same withered countenance and vacant, staring eyes as the others, but seemed out of place among the workers. His skin was particularly pale, and he wore a tattered white suit coat which had once clearly been a piece of fine clothing.

Junior replied, "Oh, just someone who owed Papa a debt." He then grinned devilishly. "A debt which has now been repaid."

Doorways to the Unseen

I was born to be a seaman, and it's all I've ever endeavored to be. From my youth and then into the first days of a looming dotage, my years were spent sailing the oceans of the world, living a life those who seek comfort and safety would never dare consider. Why should I have settled for a life unlived, never testing my true worth? Every man is born as many men, but he dies as just one.

But where shall I start this odd and unusual tale, this unbelievable encounter with things unknown and unexplainable? At the beginning, of course, where all good stories start.

I was hired as a crew member onto *The Invictus*, a newly constructed seaworthy vessel bound for trade waters charted by many previous crews and cartographers. The ship's captain, one Captain John Miles, told the new recruits he needed men who were not just brave but fearless, men who could drink death like fine wine if the occasion called for it.

Captain Miles promised the crew pay well above grade as well as a substantial bonus once we secured our cargo at the predestined unloading port on the other side of the ocean. What our cargo was, however, Captain Miles did not say, but the hint of danger was present, commensurate with our excellent salary.

The Invictus left our northern port of call along the balmy coast and sailed out into the vast ocean, passing between continents, fading from the sights of civilized men and their predilections. Our ship traveled for days without incident, making good time along our course. The crew was at ease and confident, the waters calm and accommodating.

But on the seventh day, the weather changed drastically—and not for the better. A terrible tempest seized upon us, forcing us off course and into waters absent on any map. The events that would follow this dreadful storm are so incredible, so beyond belief, that I would surely forgive you if you gave them no credence.

At first, the early evening was mild—the softly glowing sky was as clear as it had been at noontime that day. We sailed over tranquil waters as the sun began to set on the horizon, suffusing the top decks of our ship with a soothing warmth. We allowed ourselves to believe a long summer at sea lay ahead.

Then, though, dark clouds began to gather overhead. It was as if a thick, woolly canopy had been drawn over our vessel, covering the entirety of the sky. We heard thunder, and then saw flashes of lightning on the horizon. A squall on the open waters unlike any of us had ever seen would soon come upon us.

The frothing waves around our ship began to heave, and heavy rain started to fall. We tried to maintain control—Gods, we tried—but we rode the crashing waves and fierce winds like a bucking horse, wild and untamed.

The storm winds lashing around him, Captain Miles shouted above the roaring din of the rising typhoon: "Bring down the sails or they'll be torn from the masts! Quickly, men, now!"

The crew acted with utmost speed, but the high winds were far too vicious. Ocean water rushed over the decks, striking an unlucky crewman and sweeping him overboard—he was gone before any of us could even reach the rail, lost to the swirling abyss. Our once-mighty ship was but a mote in the whirlwind, dancing about the treacherous waters.

Without warning, an enormous cresting tidal wave appeared above the ship and seemed as if it would drag *The Invictus* down into a watery grave—but, instead, we were tossed away by the storm winds. The gigantic wave crashed behind the ship's stern, spraying its decks with Neptune's bile.

The force of it flung our ship from the roughest waters near the center of the tempest into considerably less turbulent seas. We glided through without sails—as the captain warned, they'd been torn away almost entirely.

The storm roiled around us for some time until it stealthily rolled back, almost as quickly as it had come. It was night, the skies above clear again, full of sparkling stars and constellations for which no charts existed.

The crew worked under the light of lanterns and hung new sails onto the square-rigged masts of our full-rigged ship. The winds were dead now, eerily still after their violent exhibition only a few hours afore.

By morning, the ocean winds had picked up again, and we sailed once more over calm waters. The crew was beginning to panic as the ship's navigator could set no course—our nautical maps were useless in these strange, uncharted waters.

The captain attempted to reassure the crew, claiming our situation was only temporary, that we would soon find our way back to land and then a friendly port. The steward checked our supplies and informed us we could not be lost for long as our surplus was limited, allowing for a few months at most.

For several days and several nights, we sailed almost blind, looking for familiar star patterns or signs of land on the horizon. But on the third night, our barrelman cried out to us, having spotted a vessel not unlike our own from the crow's nest.

The ship was a three-masted barque, hanging stationary in the distance. The captain examined the possibly derelict ship through his looking glass, the large moon overhead bathing the craft in a spectral blue light.

The translucent thing bopped on the waters, swaying as the waves dashed against its hull. Its sails were down, its decks empty of crewmen or any signs of life at all. The cold white barque seemed like a rare jewel on the dark waters of the unfamiliar sea, enticing us toward it.

The captain gave the order to board, reasoning that we locate some clue as to our whereabouts on its premises. We pulled in our ship's sails and sat still on the water. The captain, first mate, myself, and several other crewmen formed the boarding party and stood near the rail, peering over at the nearing hulk.

The crew lowered one of the ship's two gigs down the side of our vessel, and the six of us oared to our destination. A chill spread over me as our gig came to rest near the barque's starboard side. Peering up at the silent ship, I thought it a floating tomb, the resting place of dead men lost at sea.

We slowly rowed along the starboard side, examining the ship's hull with our glowing lanterns. Below the ship's bow was the carved figurehead of a beautiful woman in flowing white robes, her back arched toward the sea. The name *The Lady Cornwall* was etched in gold lettering along the side of the ship's upper hull, framing the figurehead's bare feet.

We moored against the hull and scaled the shrouds hanging loosely along its starboard side. The deck from the ship's fore to its aft was entirely empty, but a door to the decks below was open and lightless, impenetrable in the dark of night.

The captain raised his lantern before him and motioned for us to follow. We climbed slowly down the flight of stairs into the belly of the ship, finding a cabin near the stairwell whose door had also been left wide open.

It was spacious, and appeared to have belonged to the ship's captain. A porcelain cup set on its saucer was on the table, filled with brewed coffee, still warm to the touch. A map of the waters near our original port of departure lay next to it, folded open, with a ship's nautical compass and a sextant nearby.

We ventured on, peering into the other cabins, all of which showed signs of recent occupation: The crew's sleeping quarters had recently slept-in bunks, tables with playing cards laid out, as well as cooling cups of coffee and edible food on plates. The ship's galley was not bare, but instead was stocked with fresh foodstuffs. It was as if the crew had stood up amid their daily activities and walked as one out into the ocean, vanishing forever.

After a thorough search of the ship, we found nothing to inform us of our plight. The mystery of why the ship's crew had disappeared so suddenly, apparently near our departure port, felt like an omen of what would eventually befall our own ship. We resolved to find our way back to dry land and survive this test of our strength and will, to live to tell the tale I am telling you now.

First commandeering the choicest supplies for our crewmen, we unmoored our gig from *The Lady Cornwall* and rowed the small patch of ocean back to *The Invictus*. After boarding our ship, we bedded down to sleep for the remainder of the night, and hoped favorable winds would return to us in the morning. The quartermaster would account for the enigmatic ship's excess stock the following day.

I was lying in my cot that night, unable to find sleep, when I heard sails being hoisted and the night watchman cry out, "The ship, she looks about to set sail! But there's no crew about her!"

We rushed from our cabins above decks and saw full sails billowing about the masts of *The Lady Cornwall*, swollen in the cool ocean wind. The ship tilted to one side and began to sail into the darkness, away from our ship and into waters we had not yet explored. No captain or crew could be seen on the ship's upper deck—I told myself the clouded dark of the dead of night must be to blame.

The unfurled sails of *The Invictus* impelled us forward, giving chase to *The Lady Cornwall*. We followed the ghost ship over the seas, pacing behind her for at least one hour's time. What we hoped to accomplish I cannot say, but we prayed *The Lady Cornwall* might lead us to our eventual rescue . . . and not, the good Lord forbid, our doom.

The distance between *The Invictus* and *The Lady Cornwall* grew as we sailed, until the ethereal ship was but an insignificant dot on the night sea. An uncanny fog had rolled out over the surface of the ocean, darkish green in hue, as if emanating from the ghost ship itself. It grew thick and eerie, roiling about us as we sailed into its midst, dim orbs floating within its saturnine depths.

The Lady Cornwall could no longer be seen. In fact, nothing was visible save the preternatural fog that enswathed *The Invictus* like a smothering tarpaulin. We sailed into what we knew might be oblivion—there was no other recourse.

A bright light appeared in the center of the fog, directly ahead of our ship's bow. We sailed forward, grasping at this single chance to possibly break through the fog and finally find land—and it grew, eclipsing the murky shades of fog and replacing them with a radiant yellow sheen. *The Invictus* cut through the wall of fog and emerged into cleansing daylight, a warm blue-green sea stretching out in every direction. The fog behind us was gone.

There was no sign of *The Lady Cornwall*. The captain took his spyglass and searched for a coast or an island where we might find safe harbor, anywhere that promised at least temporary succor. And yes, there was something: a mountainous island with a long shoreline, perhaps but a league away.

We came to rest in the littoral waters near a sandy beach unmarred by the intrusions of men. Our ship's two gigs made several trips back and forth until most of her crew was on land, the first we had seen since departing on this mad expedition.

The island was tropical, humid, and unfavorable to men such as ourselves. Great palmed trees spanned much of its interior, while the undergrowth near the beach was dense and brushed continually against us as we strode forth to explore.

A natural path through the jungle led up the side of a steep, sloping cliff nearby. We assembled on this plateau, which offered a bird's-eye view of the island's dense interior. The many spires of an unknown city were visible to us now, set deep within the lush confines of the island's primeval jungle.

The calls of feral animals echoed over our heads as we slashed away at the ripe vines that blocked our egress, laying a passageway through the jungle inland. The tangled bush was resistant to our cutlasses but not invulnerable and, by late in the day, we'd found the outskirts of the city.

We stood on the threshold of a vast stone metropolis, bizarre in its structures and antediluvian in its appearance—a city that seemed somehow to predate humanity itself given the size of its buildings, whose inhabitants surely would have to have been giants.

But the city was empty. Not a soul could be seen as we passed its towering monuments and walked its broad avenues, long since vacated. The sound of our footsteps on stone was all that could be heard.

An enormous eye set in relief above its columnated entranceway, massive stone steps carved from volcanic rock led to a temple dedicated to forgotten gods. The unblinking, cyclopean eye seemed to burn in its resting place, though it was as cold as any other stone.

The sun was beginning to set over the island's horizon, and Captain Miles ordered the crew to make camp under the temple's edifice. Campfires dotted the smooth floors under the temple's pillars like fireflies, and a tent was erected for the captain and his first mate.

A watchman was set at the temple steps, and the men fell into slumber. I was struck by the silence—it seemed as if the nighttime sounds of the tropical wilderness could not penetrate the enclosures of the stone city, which remained uncommonly still and quiet.

Then I heard it. At first, it was only a whisper in the wind, but the awful shrieking soon grew closer. There was not one, but many of them, coming in the darkness from the temple itself, from within the lightless corridors engraved with abominable depictions of obscene rites and rituals.

Bulbous, staring eyes in the dozens; masses of glistening, grotesque flesh; trails of caustic slime spawned from the ocean's primordial ooze. The shambling horrors were upon us with ferocious speed before we could arise, tossing the crew about like ragged dolls, feeding them into gaping maws with hook-suckered tentacles.

The men who survived the savage onslaught ran from the temple into the night-shrouded city, hearing the distant screams of Captain Miles and the first mate echoing behind them.

I, with those left of our expedition, unmoored our landed gig from the shores of the beach and pushed it out into the waters. We rowed furiously back to *The Invictus*, the monstrosities howling with bloodlust as they clambered through the jungle behind us.

Now with only a skeleton crew and no captain, we drifted into the sea around the island, cursing the ill fortune that had come upon us. Even if another island refuge were found, how did we know it wouldn't also be inhabited by monsters dredged from the depths of Hell itself?

We soon spied *The Lady Cornwall* in the moonlight, coasting within a league of our ship. Why the vessel had disappeared the first time and why it now returned to us, I may never know. The ghost ship sailed through the night, passing by our ship's port side, as if inviting *The Invictus* to follow her yet again.

In our fear and madness, we pursued with no apparent purpose. She sped forward, enlarging the gap between the two ships, racing ever faster into what would become a yawning void in the ocean.

Once again out on the open ocean with no land in sight, the waters beneath us began to churn. We found we had sailed into an immense vortex, our hapless ship turning in ever-dwindling circles toward the center. *The Invictus* was pulled under by the maelstrom, sinking into the trenches of the alien ocean, taking her drowning crew with her.

In the near darkness, my lungs filling with brine, I saw a vast underwater graveyard of ships stretched out below. Some were from past ages, while others were of a like I had never before witnessed. These strange ships seemed built of solid metal from stern to bow, with no observable masts or sails.

Where I am now, I can't quite say. Some may call this place Hell, while others might name it Purgatory. I now share this ghostly ship with men from many ages and nations; we sail the seas for all time, luring seamen to their deaths beneath the waves. This is my fate, to forever remain a crewman on *The Lady Cornwall.*

About the Author

James Dermond is a writer who lives in Colorado. Intrigued from an early age by horror anthologies and the short story form, he offers this book as his latest modest contribution to the genre.

Doorways to the Unseen 12: 6 Tales of Terror and Suspense is the twelfth volume in a series of short story collections. This is the final volume in the series Doorways to the Unseen.

To sign up for free eBooks and other future giveaways, please subscribe to James Dermond's author website here:

www.jamesdermond.com

James Dermond's Amazon Author Page

https://www.amazon.com/James-Dermond/e/B01M1S54YP

James Dermond's Goodreads Author Page

https://www.goodreads.com/author/show/15862747.James_Dermond

James Dermond on Facebook

https://www.facebook.com/JamesDermondAuthor/

James Dermond on Twitter

https://twitter.com/JamesDermond

Postscript

Thank you for reading the latest volume in the short horror story series Doorways to the Unseen! This book is the twelfth in a twelve-volume series. Ambages Books plans to release a multi-volume hardcover edition of the series' collected stories in October 2026.

If you enjoyed this collection of stories, please leave a review on Amazon and other online bookstores where volumes in the Doorways to the Unseen series can be found. A positive review will help promote the book and inform other readers of the book's merits.

www.ingramcontent.com/pod-product-compliance
Lightning Source LLC
LaVergne TN
LVHW051010080826
845145LV00009B/2551

* 9 7 8 1 9 4 6 0 3 8 1 1 1 *